Open Skies

The Enforcers: book 1

A.J. Marcus

Nicole Godfrey

See what A.J. Marcus is up to.
Visit his website www.ajmarcus.com

Copyright 2018 © MysticHawker Press
http://www.mystichawker.com/

ISBN: 13-978-1-945632-53-2

Edited by Chealsea Harper
Cover design by Jodi Cox find her at www.jodicox.com

Chapter One

THE THUNDERSTORM crackled with electricity, making Theo's feathers prickle. He'd flown for what felt like hours, but still wasn't sure how far into Colorado he'd come. Daylight had filled the sky when he left Santa Fe, but the storm made it impossible to tell what time of day it was at that moment. Rolling mountains and flowing plains gave way to a gray-scale landscape drenched in rain. Ionized ozone tickled Theo's nose every time the sky lit up.

The Enforcer couldn't be far behind, not with the spectacle he'd made of himself.

Theo hoped his sacrifice would be appreciated, if not by his brother then maybe his mother. Fynn deserved the chance to grow up and feel safe.

Lightning streaked across the sky, illuminating the clouds as they roiled around him. Sure enough, Theo spotted the darker outline of a falcon in hot pursuit. The smaller bird had speed and maneuverability on his side, but Theo had power. His larger wing span pushed him through the sky, like the great Thunderbirds of legend. Every time he flew, he felt invincible. Still, he'd had a pretty sizable head start, and the fact this Enforcer had caught up with him shifted the advantage in favor of the smaller bird.

Golden Eagle or not, Theo needed to shake the falcon, or the smaller bird would overtake him shortly.

Theo changed course and winged toward a lightning cloud. His momma would tan his hide if she knew, but he couldn't see any other way to lose the man somehow tracking him through the turbulent sky.

A sphere of what looked like lightning passed by Theo's head. He glanced back over his wing in time to see the falcon shoot another ball of energy at him. He had no idea there were shifters with the ability to shoot lightning, and the revelation made his chest tighten with fear.

He swerved to miss the second attack and altered his wing position as much as the wind would allow so he could fly in a zigzag pattern. The Enforcer got off two more blasts before Theo made it to the cloud. The falcon was way too close for comfort. His confidence slipped. Maybe he wouldn't be able to lose the other bird, but he didn't have time to doubt himself.

His mother's caring face flashed through his mind. Her smile, the way she loved her two sons, and the hard work she suffered through every day to give them what they needed.

She'd be disappointed in him when she found out he was a wanted criminal. Theo plunged into the cover of the storm. Clouds closed around him starting with his beak. Claustrophobia engulfed him for several moments before he hit the air flow channels inside the swirling gray and he could see where he flew again. Ducking into the cumulous cluster closest to him, Theo spun to avoid electrical currents and stay out of the visible area where he came in.

He'd never been one to shy away from a fight, but he couldn't help but feel like avoiding confrontation would be best.

Theo wove in and out of several more pockets. Electricity sparked at random and singed his feathers, but the smell whipped away almost as quickly as it formed. He rode an air current upward and hovered close to the top of the cloud. Glancing around, Theo couldn't spot the falcon, even with all of the smaller arcs of lightning slithering between the gaps in the dark clouds. He heaved a sigh and dipped in the direction of what he hoped was the opposite side of the storm from where he entered.

Open Skies

Something flashed in front of his face and searing pain filled his right wing. Before Theo had a chance to think, the falcon dropped back down and swiped his claws across Theo's chest. He screamed in pain and flapped his wings to get away. The falcon stayed with him, clawing at Theo as he flew. Feathers flew away in all directions. Claws slashed, and the falcon screamed at the same time Theo did. Pain and instinct took over, driving Theo to lash out and defend himself.

Each hit Theo thought he made, the falcon scored at least two more. Cut after cut covered Theo, until he felt as if his entire body was on fire. They moved too close to a section of cloud with several bolts of lightning shooting out of it. The falcon flinched and pulled away from Theo's onslaught. Theo used the reprieve to grab the other bird by the talons and throw him toward the continual arcs of sparking energy. As the falcon tumbled beak over claws, a ball of energy shot out. Theo was too close to dodge and took the full blast to his injured wing.

He felt like he'd been hit with a Taser. His entire right side locked up and he couldn't control his wing. Theo tipped to one side. He flapped his left wing in an attempt to compensate, but couldn't keep altitude. Theo tried instead to let his good wing slow his descent. That was when he realized another mass fell with him not too far away. He could make out wings, but couldn't see the face of the falcon. Theo moved his wing to get closer, but couldn't maneuver effectively.

Fear and panic gripped Theo at the thought of the falcon's unconscious body hitting the ground. He didn't wish the shifter any harm. The Enforcer was just doing his job, after all.

Buzzing filled his head and he lost track of the falling falcon. He knew his energy slowly drained from multiple wounds. He needed to find a rural place to land and shift.

The effects of the energy blast were wearing off. Part of being a golden eagle shifter was having healing properties in his blood. Scientists in the shifter community tried to synthesize the effects but failed due to the other property that came with it. Golden eagle blood also had hallucinogenic properties. The two effects were intertwined and proved impossible for science to separate. Apparently. Theo was grateful for the gift either way, and awkwardly flew away from the lightning cloud. Somehow, he managed to force his injured wing to open enough that he could glide along the currents of the storm and ride them without continuing his plummet toward the ground. His internal compass took him north, away from the storm and the injured Enforcer.

By the time the sun peeked over the eastern horizon, Theo forgot everything but pain. He couldn't think of why he flew on or why he hovered over a dense, green forest. Hadn't there been a storm of some kind? Wasn't there another bird? And didn't the trees below look like the best place in the world to sleep? He circled down, coming in at an odd angle and hitting the branches twined together in the canopy. His injured wing still wasn't completely responsive. The left side of his body was sluggish. He reached his claws out to get purchase on something, but they wouldn't listen to him and kept slipping off limbs and trunks. The ground came up to meet him in a cloud of disturbed dirt and loose plumage, but he barely felt the impact.

The air smelled funny, like rotting leaves and something sweet. If he could just shift, all of his burning cuts would heal. Or if he had a tongue like a dog, he could lick his wounds and get the full benefits of his blood. Even if it caused him to trip out for a bit, it would be a far cry better than the constant pain. Theo couldn't pull his wings in or shuffle over to the closest tree for cover. He'd only missed landing in a bush by a foot or so, but he still felt way too exposed.

If he could only rest his eyes for a few moments…Surely his mama would tell him to rest. He drifted off on a sea of throbbing pain and burning muscles as a pool of sunlight bathed him in warmth.

Soft crunching woke him from blissful oblivion. Warm light covered the nearby bushes and left him in cold shadows. More crunching and rustling came from somewhere close, but Theo couldn't look to see where exactly. A pair of tightly laced combat boots stopped next to his head. He glanced up, but the owner of said boots was only a silhouette against the light.

"Well now. Here's a mess I didn't want to find today, or any day for that matter. Where did you come from? And why didn't I see you coming in the first place?" The man's voice had an interesting accent. One that Theo wasn't familiar with.

The man's crazy talk about seeing Theo coming could've been muddling things, or perhaps he was still exhausted in spite of his nap. Theo tested to see if he could move and every fiber of his being screamed in protest. He must have made a noise because the man knelt down.

"You really shouldn't be moving. I know you can understand me, so please don't try to move." He sighed. "I guess this means I'll have to take you home with me. If I leave you here to fend for yourself, you could die. I can't allow that to happen."

Theo would've rolled his eyes if he physically could.

The man gingerly scooped Theo up out of the dirt. "So much for my quiet walk."

Chapter Two

JAMES CHAN frowned as he carried the wounded eagle shifter through the forest he called home. It had been years since the outside world last impeded on his peace and quiet. He kept his own trips into Billings as infrequent as possible. His precognitive abilities used to warn him if he was going to run into trouble so he could sidestep things he didn't want to deal with. It'd been a long time since the gifts of his Tengu ancestors first failed him. This eagle would cause him problems. He felt sure of it, although he couldn't tell for sure what kind of problems or how it would affect him. Not knowing the answers tore at James' still wounded soul. What made him so sure of trouble to come, in place of his abilities, was the fact he carried a male eagle toward his home. Taking home stray men always spelled trouble.

The ten pounds of feathers and bones seemed to weigh more and more as he carried it through the woods. The burden was a bit much for his outstretched arms.

"I know you can understand me, well if you speak English. If you speak a different language, you need to let me know. I speak several. I'm going to move you closer to my body and fold up your wings. If that hurts, I'm sorry. Do me a favor and don't foot me. I'll remember if you do and will balance the scales as soon as you're well." James slowly folded the eagle's wings in, the left one resisted a bit and made him suspect there was an injury there. The bird's eyes were clouded and unfocused. He wondered about head trauma, but didn't know of anyone he could take a shifter to for doctoring. They didn't usually need medical attention unless they were gravely injured, which this one appeared to be.

For the first time in years, he wished he was still a member of the Enforcers. He could've used their resources to find help for the kid. Even covered in feathers, James knew the eagle he carried was younger than he was. In human years he'd give the man under the down maybe twenty five, but he doubted any older. The Enforcers had people they could put folks in touch with, but when he left them, he'd faked his own death and vowed to never return under any circumstances. He'd just have to trust his instincts and do what he could to help the kid pull through.

"We're almost there." James huffed as they topped the ridge that looked down on his cabin. The mountains around his home provided him plenty of exercise, whether it was hiking or flying. It kept him in good shape, but toting the wounded eagle nearly three miles over uneven terrain took a toll. His arms and shoulders ached as he started down the well-trodden path to his door.

The cabin was small, just one bedroom, the main room, a bathroom and the root cellar. He didn't worry about any of the local grizzlies invading his space. He had an understanding with them. They left did bother him and he left them alone. Even the wild eagles gave his territory a wide berth, which was how he liked it.

He bent awkwardly to open the unlocked door. The key to the doorknob had been lost years ago, but he didn't need to lock things up.

Carrying the eagle into the bedroom, he laid him down carefully before he turned on the light. He also picked up a flashlight. Back at the bed, he opened the eagle's eyes and shined the light in. Both eyes were slow to respond.

James shook his head and set the flashlight on the nightstand. "Yep, you've definitely got some head trauma there buddy. It might be a little while before you can shift. I'm going to get some water for you. Do me a favor and don't shit on the bed. I don't have a lot of bedding and it takes time for slices to dry before they flake out easily. "

The big bird looked at him with unfocused eyes. There was something in that gaze that touched James. He couldn't put a name to it, but he didn't like the feeling. He vowed as soon as the stranger had his strength back he'd send him on his way. James didn't want any problems, and weird sensations, combined with his precognitive powers failing to alert him to trouble, insinuated a bigger mess than he cared to think about. When his gifts didn't show him something, that meant it was something he couldn't avoid in the first place. He never liked destiny knocking on his door.

He turned the light off as he walked out of the bedroom, heading down to the root cellar. He wanted to see if he had enough food for the two of them or if he needed to go out and catch something. He paused in the living room and turned on his computer. One of the few amenities he allowed himself was the internet. If it hadn't been for the satellite connection, he wouldn't have bothered, but he wanted to check and see if he could find out anything about a missing eagle. Ourotherselves.net would be his starting point. When he'd left the Enforcers, the social networking site and database had just gotten started. He knew it was a long shot since not all the shifters were on it. A good number of them didn't even know about it. But it might help him figure out who the kid was. The idea of waiting until his head was together enough to shift irritated James.

As his computer booted up he continued on to the root cellar. Opening the freezer, he frowned. There was still some meat left from the moose he'd taken down the previous fall, but there wasn't a lot of it. He had a few rabbits in single serving sizes. Taking two of the Ziploc bags out, he returned to the cabin and left them on the kitchen counter. He'd debate what to fix with them later.

James checked in on the injured eagle shifter. He was still lying on the bed, apparently asleep. With severe head trauma, sleep was debatable. There was a school of thought to keep the patient awake for a long period of time to make sure the brain didn't swell too much and kill them while they were unconscious. Although James didn't bear the man any ill, he wasn't so concerned with his well-being as to make the effort to keep him awake. The fact that he was a shifter also made things a little less cut and dried. Their healing worked faster and different than humans or eagles.

With an eagle shifter, healing was even more complex. James didn't think letting the man sleep would be a problem.

He settled at his computer and pulled up his browser. A headline on Ourotherselves.net caught his attention. A human was attacked by an eagle in Santa Fe. James paused and looked toward the bedroom. He was a long way from New Mexico. The eagle would've had to fly all day and night to make it to his quiet mountainside. It didn't make a lot of sense, particularly with the injuries he had. But then if he'd attacked a human and received those injures, the human wasn't a normal human. A magic user, maybe, but not a normal human.

James jumped on the groups for avian shifters, trying to see if anyone was claiming to know anything. Everything was quiet. The most recent eagle shifter disappearance was almost a year ago, and that one had been a middle-aged woman in Texas. Nothing in his part of the country. He didn't want to risk drawing attention to himself, so he didn't post asking if anyone was missing an eagle in the Montana area. He could find out more if and when the man woke. He closed the browser and checked his email. Only a few people had his email address. He didn't really expect anything.

With a heavy sigh, James stood and strolled over to his bay window that looked out onto the rolling meadow below the cabin. He didn't normally have to force his precognitive powers to get them to work, but the inner quiet disturbed him. Sitting in his peaceful place, he closed his eyes and reached out to see what waited for him in the future.

Pushing his senses out, he tried to pierce the veil between the present and the future. At first, nothing happened. Then feathers floated down around him. There were a lot of them. Dark brown eagle feathers, black raven feathers, gray and white falcon feathers. It was like a storm of feathers spiraling about him. He reached out and grabbed one of the eagle feathers. Blood discolored the tip of it, dark, red, and wet. In the distance an owl cackle sounded almost like a laugh. He struggled to understand what it meant. Normally his visions were a lot clearer. He was used to seeing who, when and where. This vision didn't help him at all. It confused him. There wasn't anything firm in it. He tossed the feather away and it zipped back to the ring of feathers spinning around him.

A soft flapping sound came from the bedroom, breaking into his meditative state. James jumped up and dashed for the room. Hopefully the eagle wasn't hurting himself.

Chapter Three

THE WALLS were wrong. His mother's trailer on the outskirts of Santa Fe had faux wood panels, not solid wood lacquered to a glossy finish. The pungent, intoxicating smell of man filled Theo's nostrils and when he tried to move, pain radiated through his body. His feathers rustled and reminded him that he was still in eagle form.

Panic filled him with energy he never should've had in his delirious state. He flapped his wing through the pain, trying with all his might to shift back to human.

Footsteps sounded with hollow thuds nearby. A door opened and a man appeared. He held up his hands and approached the bed. "That's not going to do you any good. You're only hurting yourself."

Theo recognized the voice and the man's smell matched that of the bed. Foggy memories surfaced. This man brought Theo here…from the forest. There was another bird. A falcon. And—*Oh!* It all came back in a rush. His brother, the attack, and taking the heat. The whole time his thoughts were rushing by like a train, he continued to struggle. He had to get back to his human self. He had to be able to talk.

"Please stop that!" The man cussed under his breath and stepped forward. "Don't make me hold you down."

That snapped Theo out of his panic. He stopped trying to move his wings and rested on the bed, panting.

With a big sigh, the man came to sit beside Theo on the bed. "I'm glad you can be reasonable."

He preferred calm, but there was no way to convey that.

The man rubbed his face. "What the hell are you doing, James? Why can't you let this kid take care of himself? You don't even know his name."

Theo fully intended on taking care of himself, just as soon as he could shift and get things back to where they should be.

"I wish you could shift, so I could ask you your name. Don't suppose you could give me some kind of sign that you're doing better?" He raised an eyebrow at Theo.

Theo offered his rescuer a feeble squawk.

James adjusted on the bed and reached for Theo's wing. "I'll take that as a kinda sorta."

The hand reaching for his wing made Theo nervous. He pulled back from the contact and let out another pathetic cry.

"You're going to have to trust me. I promise I won't hurt you." James held his hands where they were, as if waiting.

The look in James' eyes combined with the twinge of pain made Theo stop moving. He tilted his head, keeping James' hands in his line of sight. After a few moments where no one moved, James gingerly touched the injured wing. The contact wasn't enough to cause Theo discomfort, but he still cringed in anticipation.

James' brow furrowed as he explored. "I'm no vet, but I think our best bet is to bind this up. It will probably hurt like the dickens."

He tilted his head at James again, hoping it would convey his assent.

Leaving for several moments and returning with first-aid material, James mumbled to himself, "I guess I should be more prepared. You can't always get to a vet when you're hurt, especially in eagle form."

Though another element of strain arose, some part of Theo relaxed at the thought of being with another shifter. It also meant that James wasn't insane for talking to a bird.

"I wish I had something to numb this, but I don't even have Oral gel—wait!" James walked out with the snap of his fingers.

James seemed a little scattered, like he wasn't used to having someone in his space. Sure, everyone liked their privacy at times, but Theo had his mom and Fynn to share space with. Family made alone time harder to come by.

Wearing a broad smile and carrying a bag of ice, James strolled back into the room. "It's not much, but at least it will lessen the pain. I'll hold it so there isn't unnecessary pressure on your wing. Just hold still for me."

Theo braced himself, holding his breath to stop from screeching when the cold bag touched him.

True to his word, James kept the bag from weighing his wing down. The cold swept through his limb, blissfully removing the ache. James kept the bag in place long enough for a comfortable numbness to settle in. Then James pushed the wing closed and pressed it to Theo's body. He wrapped an ace bandage around Theo's torso, leaving his uninjured wing free to move. The whole process caused Theo very little discomfort, and having the wing bound seemed to help.

"That should about do it. Even without pain meds, you should heal fast enough to make a full recovery. I don't know exactly why you're here, and I'm not sure I want to, but you have my guarantee that you'll be safe until you can manage on your own." His words didn't quite inspire confidence, but they at least rang true.

Theo spent the rest of the day in and out of a doze. James moved him out into the main area of the house, either to keep an eye on him or make it so that Theo didn't feel alone. Theo liked to think it was the latter. Most of the time he was awake, James was on his computer. Curiosity burned Theo, driving him to distraction thinking about what exactly James did while clicking his little mouse.

The smell of incense pulled Theo out of a fitful sleep. Pungent Nag Champa, like the kind Theo's mom used, filled the air in wisps of smoke. The room connected to the small kitchen, so there wasn't a lot of space. James sat on the floor very close to the chair where Theo rested. He had his hands beneath him, holding his weight up off of the ground. His eyes were closed and he looked for all intents and purposes like he was completely at ease.

The amount of discipline required to maintain the pose, without any outward evidence of strain, must've taken years to obtain. Which made Theo question how old James was. Then all the clues made sense. The dark hair, the shape of his eyes, and even the indiscernible age. Though James lacked some of the stereotypical features of an Asian man, he definitely had some in his lineage. Feeling foolish for not spotting things sooner, Theo lingered on the question of whether or not James was single. More than he wanted to admit in fact.

James turned, settling himself on the floor at the same time. "Ah, you're awake. I plan on making some rabbit stew, though that may be a bit difficult for you to eat in your current state. Any chance you can shift? Not that I want to chance you making matters worse."

Theo tested the limited motion of his free wing. There was some discomfort, but not near as much as earlier in the day. He tried to push himself to support his weight with his legs and fell off the chair with a thud. A few feathers floated in the air as he looked up into James' face.

"You're right, that was too much to ask for this soon." He picked Theo up with nothing but his fingertips. Those same fingertips lingered over Theo's feathers.

Theo closed his eyes and waited for James to pull his hand away. He took longer to do so than Theo thought, but he felt no desire to bite James for petting him. In fact, he rather enjoyed the contact.

When James did finally pull away, he stepped back as Theo opened his eyes. "Yeah...yeah, I'll make the soup for me and bring you a rabbit haunch."

A rumble shook Theo's stomach at the mention of food. The sway of James' hips kept his attention and he cocked his head to the side to watch James move around the kitchen with practiced ease.

If it had been any other circumstances, Theo would've offered to help make dinner. Under any other circumstances, he would've told James he'd give anything to show appreciation for being rescued. If it had been any other circumstances, Theo never would've had the chance to meet James. And something told him that not meeting this man would be a tragedy far beyond taking the blame for something he didn't do.

James kept his back toward the living room area. Theo couldn't help but wonder if the avoidance was deliberate or not. Soon the savory smell of cooking meat overpowered the leftover scent of the strong incense. Another rumble vibrated through Theo's stomach. He would've groaned if he'd been in human form. James moved with such fluidity for performing a mundane task like cooking that Theo wanted to groan for reasons other than hunger, too.

Sitting there in a blanket nest, following the movements of one of the most attractive men he'd ever seen, Theo began to accept more and more that he'd been put in his current predicament for a reason.

Chapter Four

JAMES PERCHED on a boulder overlooking a wide valley. With the strange eagle convalescing in his cabin, he knew he needed a bit more food. Sick eagle shifters, like sick humans, required a lot of extra calories. In some ways more, due to a faster metabolism. He wasn't ready to dive into his winter stores and prey was easy enough to find. In the short time he'd perched on the rock, he'd already amassed two cottontails who'd wandered into view, and couldn't get away before he swooped down on them. But if he could get a snowshoe hare, he'd be set for a few days. They should be active, so he only had to wait.

Hunting also helped him get his mind off the constant dread that his unexpected guest would bring trouble back into his life. James had paid a high price for his solitude. Already there were drastic changes in his daily routine. He'd kept up with recent chatter in the forums instead of patrolling his land, but so far hadn't found anything interesting beyond the Albuquerque incident. Something about the attack didn't sit right, but the past wasn't his realm. Still, having some of his old contacts with the Enforcers would've been helpful. He didn't want to open that can of worms again if he didn't have to. Information could be found in other ways, he just hadn't discovered them yet.

Something moved in the valley. James pushed all other thoughts out of his head and focused his attention on the movement. A large snowshoe hare moved cautiously out of the tree line and into the lush green meadow. Knowing how fast the hare could run, James forced himself to wait. He wanted the meal, but didn't want to chase it willy-nilly through the trees if it bolted too soon. The sun sat in the right spot so it wouldn't cast a shadow when he stooped toward the hare. Finally the rabbit loped far enough from the trees and James launched himself from the boulder. He flew up before dropping down as fast as he could. The wind whistled past him while he folded his wings in tight and pumped them quickly to gain more speed as he plummeted toward his goal. Nothing could be done about the sound of wind whistling across his feathers.

At the last second, the hare looked up. It jumped and took off. James angled his tail and flew toward the fleeing brown form. As he extended his talons, his speed dropped just a bit, but his momentum carried him forward. He lost himself in the adrenaline rush of the chase with practiced ease. Pursuing prey always made him feel more alive. As an eagle shifter he was built for the hunt. James flew over the hare and grabbed its head at the perfect moment. His needle-sharp talons plunged deep through its skull, making the kill instantaneous.

The hare's momentum carried them forward a few more feet, with its hind legs flipping up and hitting James's wings. The impact caused him to tumble and roll into the grass with his prize still clutched tightly. When James stopped moving he stood, shaking off the grass and dirt from his less-than-stellar landing.

Although the hunt always made his blood race, James never hunted for fun, only for food. The thought of someone waiting back at his cabin for him to provide brought on a sudden swell of happiness. He missed having a family to care for.

Not wanting to wait for other predators or scavengers to come by, James grabbed hold of the hare and leapt into the sky. Burdened by the hare's weight, it took more effort than normal for James to fly. Being a shifter made the challenge slightly less than a oneform eagle would've had, but only marginally. As he came over the final rise between his cabin and the meadow, he realized it had been a while since he'd really challenged himself. His life in hiding had become so routine. If it hadn't been for the incredible scenery and the beautiful simplicity of it all, he'd have been bored out of his mind. His family didn't even know he was still alive, and the simple life lessened the ache in his soul. Still, the lack of complications sometimes made things too...dull.

He landed at the shed near his cabin, shifted to his human form, and scooped up all three rabbits. It was warm enough, he didn't go find a pair of pants to put on, and he didn't worry about any of his neighbors coming up on him. The closest human neighbor was a good three miles away with acres of national forest between them. Bears didn't care if he was clothed or not. He loved the isolation of it all. He could be the shifter so many city shifters wished they could be. Wild and free.

He put the snowshoe hare on the cutting block next to the two cottontails he'd caught. His skill with a blade made cleaning the rabbits quick and easy. Before long he carried the fresh meat into the house.

As he strolled through the living room, he glanced at the eagle sleeping on his couch. James frowned at the bound wing. The healing process should be complete. They were on their second day since he'd found the eagle. Something worked against them. He wondered if the other shifter had a mental block against healing. If he didn't want to heal, that might cause a big delay. But he couldn't imagine why someone wouldn't want to heal, unless they had something to hide.

James put the cleaned snowshoe hare on the cabinet and, once he had the two cottontails wrapped and in the fridge, he used choice seasonings and put it in the oven. A slow bake would make an excellent dinner. With a smile James booted up his computer.

On the main page for Ourothersleves.net there was an official post from the Enforcers about the wanted eagle in New Mexico. James stared at the posting for a minute. They'd never used things like that when he'd been part of the Enforcers. The agents working the case must not be having any luck in finding their man…or eagle as the case was…and must've been desperate for a lead. He knew if he'd been working the case, he'd use whatever resources he could to bring the perp to justice. An attack on humans was just stupid, particularly in bird form. They risked exposing the shifter community to humans. Attacking the guy with a gun made more sense, or even just a club or baseball bat. But James had seen a lot of stupid things in his days as an Enforcer.

He checked the forums for any good leads. For a moment he started feeling like an Enforcers again.

There was a certain thrill he got from chasing down the bad guys. Like the snowshoe hare. A bit more of a challenge than what his life had become over the past few years.

Most of the forums hadn't had any new information from when he'd searched the previous night. There was a bit of fuss over the Enforcer's post. Several hawk and falcon shifters sounded nervous that, if they couldn't find an eagle, the Enforcers would begin putting pressure on other raptors in hopes someone knew something. The idea made James laugh. Unless things had changed dramatically since he'd left the Enforcers, they wouldn't muscle in on the wrong species. That's not how they used to work anyway.

A rustling of feathers behind James drew his attention away from the computer to the couch. Dark eyes stared at him.

James swiveled in his computer chair, suddenly reminded that he was still naked. He often went days during the summer without wearing clothes and he'd forgotten to put anything on after hunting. A lot of shifters didn't mind nudity, but there was no way of knowing how his patient had been raised and James didn't want to make him uncomfortable. "So you're awake." He stood and hurried to the bedroom to grab a pair of sweats.

The eagle's gaze followed his movements. James wondered, not for the first time, what the young man under the feathers would look like. There were a few things that transferred between human and animal forms, like general condition. A chubby shifter would be overweight in both human and animal form, although due to their metabolism, shifters had to really work at being overweight. He had little doubt the man within would be in good shape, but beyond that, he had no clue. Bird shifters were notoriously hard to pin human characteristics to. His own black-haired Asian heritage didn't show in his eagle form. Wolves, dogs, horses and other animals which had a wide variance in color often hinted at what their human forms might look like.

Slipping his sweats on, James hurried back to the living room. "Are you feeling better today?"

The eagle on the couch blinked at him. He roused slightly, ruffling the feathers on his back and head, then his eyes drooped.

"Kinda hard to do that all bound up, isn't it?" James returned to his seat at the computer, but stayed facing the bird. "I'm hoping you'll feel good enough to shift today. If you can do that, your wing will mend…and we can talk." He sighed. Too much of their language in bird form was in body posturing and feather movements for him to get a real response to his statement. "With you trussed up like that we can't even talk as eagles."

The eagle drooped a bit as if it had the same thought.

"Hey, I caught a snowshoe hare while you were sleeping. I've got it slow roasting in the oven. It'll make a great dinner." Just talking to the bird made James's mood lighten. He'd never realized how much he missed having people to talk with. The lack of people was one of the few downsides to his isolated life, and it only hit him from time to time.

"Tell you what, why don't we head out and hang on the porch for a while? It's a pretty day and the sunshine on your feathers might do you some good." James walked over and carefully picked the bird up and carried him and the blanket nest out and set him on a large wooden barrel where he could get plenty of sun. James could take the opportunity to do a bit of stretching and exercises outside for a while.

As he worked out, James kept shooting quick glances at the eagle. The bird's gaze never left him. It was almost enough to answer his wondering if the other shifter was interested in him, but he'd wait until they could actually talk about things before…before what? He felt a pull when he looked into the eagle's eyes. Something was there, something he'd never felt before. But he didn't need anyone in his life full-time. The other man was just passing through. Even if he was interested, it would just be a quick fling and they'd go their separate ways. James didn't want anything close to a family again. Families and close companions opened people up to pain and he never wanted to endure that kind of pain again. He'd lost everything once before, and he'd vowed then he'd never let himself return to that sort of life. He didn't need anything more than his quiet life in the forest. He repeated the statement over and over again in his head, like a prayer.

Chapter Five

THEO'S GAZE followed the flow of muscle beneath skin with each move James made. He felt a rush of heat every time James glanced his way.

If he changed back to human and they talked, James would know the truth and Theo wouldn't blame him if he didn't want Theo around anymore. Facing the possibility of never seeing James again made Theo want to stay in eagle form as long as possible. But knowing James was a shifter too made coming up with a logical excuse more difficult.

He would have to face the music. Sooner rather than later. And maybe he could get to know James better if he stopped dragging his feet.

Almost as if he could feel that Theo had made a decision, James brought all of his limbs close to his body and bowed before turning toward the porch. Theo's feathers prickled.

"Sun feels good, doesn't it?" James turned a smile up toward the sky. He seemed so relaxed in that moment, so at home, that it stirred a longing inside Theo.

Theo sighed, picturing himself in human form and slipping his arm around James' waist. What he wouldn't give to share a small piece of that contentment, even for a moment.

"See you could be out here with me, feeling the sun on your skin, if you'd just try to shift back," James urged. There was an easy gentleness to it.

Was James a telepath? Theo shivered at the thought. James had an uncanny way of reacting as if he'd heard Theo's thoughts.

James walked up to the barrel Theo lay on. "What do you say? Can you give it a try?"

A tempting smile spread across James' face, but it only amplified the terror welling up from the pit of Theo's stomach. If James was indeed a telepath, he knew everything. Every dirty little detail that crossed Theo's mind. Including how many times he'd fantasized about James, especially after seeing him walk around in all of his smooth-skinned glory. Theo tilted his head away from James' scrutiny. The sun wasn't the only thing making him hot, so he tried to focus on the amazingly wild smell the place had. The pine mingled with the bracken and the clean air. The whole effect was quite urban free. No exhaust, no industrial pollution, or psychotic city crime. The more time Theo spent outside, the more he understood the draw of living in such isolation.

A gentle touch over the feathers of Theo's neck brought his momentary avoidance back to the subject at hand.

"Hey there, come on. You won't know if it'll help until you try." James' words were thick and sweet as honey, pouring liquid heat into Theo's core.

With so many reasons to say no, each more selfish than the last, Theo couldn't deny the inevitable any longer. He opened his beak and peered at James with one large eye. Nodding, James pulled at the bandage and unraveled it from around Theo's body. Once removed, and the injured wing left to hold itself, Theo chanced extending his feathers with cautionary slowness. His muscles were stiff and flying would be difficult for a time, but the massive amount of pain was no longer an issue.

Looking up at James' beaming approval, Theo closed his eyes. He promised himself that he'd be completely honest with any questions James asked him and reached for his human form. There was no resistance, as if part of him had been waiting for the moment to take hold. His balance tilted as he expanded faster than usual and he toppled off of the barrel. He landed a few feet from the porch in a tangle of limbs instead of feathers.

Soft cursing came from the direction he last saw James, then strong arms circled around his bare waist and steadied him as he stood.

"That'll teach me. Next time, put the bird on the ground before you ask them to shift." James pulled Theo upright and supported all of his weight. "Are you alright…Hey, now you can tell me what to call you."

Clearing his throat, and trying to ignore his nudity beside the shorter man, Theo looked James in the eye. "Thank you, for saving me. My name is Theo Montoya, no jokes please."

"Jokes? About what?" James' brow furrowed.

"I know my parents didn't name me Indigo, but still." Theo smiled.

James simply shook his head.

"Seriously? You've never seen The Princess Bride? Or read the book?" Theo thought everyone had at least heard of it.

"I don't watch movies, and even though my family lived in the states since before I was born, they were pretty traditional. Movies were a waste of time. I had schooling, martial arts, and…um, other kinds of training that took precedence." James glanced down, making no attempts to hide his assessing gaze.

"Um, okay then, how about some clothes for the naked shifter?" Theo resisted the urge to cover his crotch with one hand, since it was a bit late to be modest.

A smile tugged at the corner of James' thin lips, but the twinkle in his eyes was unmistakable. "Alright. I wear pretty loose fitting sweats, they should fit you."

Theo nodded and tried not to wobble. James managed to help him into the cabin and then settled him on the couch before disappearing down the hall to the bedroom. When James returned holding a rugged pair of gray sweats up to inspect, Theo shot to his feet and swayed.

"Whoa. Careful now. You may not be completely stable on your feet yet." James stepped closer, as if to grab Theo again.

Holding up his hand, Theo widened his stance to make standing easier. He had to show James he could move around on his own.

James shrugged and handed over the pants. "They aren't new, but they're clean."

Theo took the proffered clothing by the waistband and checked the tag. Medium. They'd be tight, but should fit. He looked back at James, who hadn't moved and stood there with his hands on his hips.

"Excuse me. I think I'll head to the bathroom. It's the door across from the bedroom, right? Okay." Theo didn't wait for James to finish moving before he slipped by. He could've sworn he heard a chuckle just as he closed the door behind him.

He hoped James wouldn't mind, but he needed to bathe. So he started the water and smiled at the lingering scents from all the soaps, which were the obvious source of James' unique smell. The water was gloriously hot and the shampoo felt great on his scalp as he scrubbed his short hair. Then he lathered his body, trying to avoid thoughts of a naked James as he washed his groin. When he finished, he rubbed a plush towel over his skin to sop up the extra water and glanced longingly at the single toothbrush on the shelf.

Surprisingly enough, putting the pants on didn't resolve Theo's discomfort as much as he'd hoped. The tight fit didn't leave much to the imagination, either from the front or back. He stood back from the sink, turning from side to side, the lines of his frown deepening with each pass. There were light marks across his brown flesh, mostly healed scratches from his fight with the falcon. He had no real way to hide them, and hoped they wouldn't be questioned. His chest was bare, and wearing one of James' too-small shirts would've made Theo feel like a skank. More than anything, he prayed not to get aroused in such tight fitting pants. Odd thought, but it seemed to win in favor over the battle scars.

Theo rubbed his hands over his biceps in the cooler air outside the bathroom. Sounds of clanging came from the kitchen and Theo hesitated to put himself back in James' presence. There would be immediate questions, and he wasn't sure he was ready to answer them. But the tantalizing aroma of roasting hare drew him closer. He loved food, especially his mom's, and his stomach growled in response to the idea of a cooked meal.

Just like the night before, James moved around the kitchen with ease, but this time he chopped potatoes and tossed them into a pot of water on the stove.

"Ahem. Thank you for the use of your shower, the hot water was nice." Theo tucked his thumbs in the waistband of the sweats.

James turned and looked Theo up and down. "The sweats suit you. So does the lack of a shirt. You must stay pretty active."

Not exactly the inquiry he'd expected, but he answered truthfully. "I have a younger brother, and it takes a bit to keep up with teenagers."

"A teen, huh?" James turned back to chopping potatoes.

Cursing himself for the slip, Theo hurried to lead the topic away from Fynn. "Well, it would probably be just as taxing to keep up with toddlers. Do you have any younger siblings?"

A half peeled potato hit the floor and rolled toward the back door. James scooped it up before it could stop moving. He didn't say anything until he shut the water off from rinsing the fallen spud.

"No, I don't have any family." The comment was laden with hidden meaning, even to a not-at-all psychic like Theo.

Family seemed to be off the discussion table for both of them, then. Theo decided against pushing the issue and cleared his throat. "Hey, my mom says I'm a pretty good assistant in the kitchen. Is there something I can do to help?"

"There's a peeler in that drawer," he said, pointing to the top drawer to his left. "Go ahead and peel while I cut."

Happy to be helping, Theo retrieved the peeler and started on the next washed potato on the counter. James wielded the knife like a master chef, chopping like a fiend. The motions were so fast Theo had a hard time following them.

"You're amazing with a blade. Is that from your martial arts training?" Theo wished his brother could be there. Fynn would have loved to watch the skills in action.

"Partially." James said in a low tone.

Theo continued to peel while a somewhat tense silence filled the air.

"At least you're up and moving around. If we can get you back in the air without falling like a rock, you should be good to go about your business. I'm sure your mom and brother will be missing you terribly." James didn't stop what he was doing as he spoke.

"Probably, but I can't go home right now." Theo braced himself for the expected fifty questions.

"Hmm, that's too bad. I'm sure you have more important things to do either way." He pushed the potatoes off the cutting board into the boiling water. "Could you finish these up? I need to check for a work email I've been waiting for."

"Sure, I guess I can do that." Theo didn't want James to leave his side. In spite of the awkward conversation, he was enjoying the company. Even in high school Theo had a hard time making friends. This was the first time he'd gotten into comfortable, yet awkward, banter since he'd tried to go to a shifter social. He knew very little about James, but the one thing neither of them had to hide was what they were. What *did* James feel he needed to hide?

Chapter Six

JAMES GLANCED at the kitchen and Theo as he waited for the internet page to load. He didn't remember a name being mentioned in the eagle attack post, but he wanted to make sure. He knew it was being stereotypic, but with a name like Theo Montoya, the kid could've come from New Mexico. Flying from Santa Fe to Montana would've been taxing at best. The flight would've explained why Theo had been so worn out. It didn't explain his injuries, but a rough storm and being overly tired would lend itself to a shifter being damaged when trying to land, or avoid an obstacle. The mostly healed scratches on his chest screamed of a fight with another shifter, but having a younger sibling could explain them as well. Anything was possible really.

He found the post and scanned it. No names. He frowned. If he still had access to the Enforcers' resources, he could've looked up Theo in their database and known almost everything about him. But he didn't. There was something about him that made James think he wasn't the type to attack a human, not without extenuating circumstances.

"Anything beyond potatoes?" Theo asked from the kitchen.

James closed down his browser. "Nope, now we just let it all simmer for a while." He pulled up his email and was a little relieved there wasn't anything new.

Theo leaned against the kitchen counter and folded his arms across his broad chest, covering most of the healing scratches. James realized that unless he was just going to loan the kid jackets and tight sweats to wear, he'd need to go into Billings and get Theo a couple changes of clothes or face days of having to wrench his eyes away from the brawny sight before him. He was just small enough his shirts wouldn't fit the handsome Hispanic.

"So, do we need to sit in here and watch the pots boil, or can we go back out on the porch?" Theo sounded a bit nervous as he uncrossed and re-crossed his arms.

Unable to tell if he was trying to hide the scratches, or just being jittery, James shrugged. "It'll take the potatoes a little while. We can go outside. The smoke alarm will let us know if anything catches fire." He chuckled softly at his own joke. "It's a nice day out. Maybe we can see how well you can fly."

A soft shudder passed through Theo. "Then shouldn't we shift inside first?"

"You're a city shifter aren't you? We're out in the middle of nowhere. Nobody's going to see us." James got out of his computer chair and headed for the door. "Come on."

The warm wind ruffled his hair as he walked out and let his sweats fall to the ground. It felt good. Even after his earlier hunting, James welcomed the easy sensation of shifting and letting the wind course through his feathers. He equated the feeling to wiggling toes in sand or walking barefoot on grass. Thankful his shifts flowed like water, he jumped off the ground and flapped a couple of times, quickly getting to the top of the aspens that ringed the clearing around the cabin.

Glancing over his shoulder, Theo stood on the porch, just watching. If he'd had lips, James would've frowned. He turned on a wing tip and swooped toward the cabin.

An odd look appeared on Theo's face as James landed on the water barrel and gave him a short scream of encouragement. His brows were knitted together, lips pursed, and he kept glancing down. James looked at him, and for a moment wished he had some level of telepathy, like a few of the elite Enforcers had. At least it would've helped him get through to Theo that he wanted to fly.

Theo shook his head. "Sorry. I guess after spending a couple of days in my eagle form, it just feels good to be human for a little while."

Standing straight and maintaining a lot of control over his shift so he wouldn't tumble off the barrel like Theo had, James willed himself back to human. "You really *are* a city shifter, aren't you?" Over the years he'd met a lot of shifters who were more comfortable in their human skin than their true forms. He never really understood it. They all had two forms and should revel in them, not fight against the animal side.

"Yeah." Theo sat on the edge of the porch. "I mean, don't get me wrong, I love it out here. This forest and these mountains are great. It's just that was the longest I think I've ever spent in bird form. I was getting a bit concerned there might be something wrong and I was stuck."

Not bothering to get his sweats from the doorway where he'd left them, James hopped off the barrel and walked over to sit next to Theo. "How often do you shift at home?"

Theo shrugged. "A couple times a week, if I'm lucky. We have to be careful with everything. We don't want Enforcers breathing down our necks if we get caught."

James pursed his lips. He knew how the Enforcers got when they thought someone had accidentally exposed the shifter world to the humans. They'd killed people for impractical shifting and other things that involved a lot of cover-up. Staying out of the view of the Enforcers was the biggest reason he lived so remotely.

"That sucks. I understand keeping away from the Enforcers." He patted Theo's leg. "At least while you're here, you don't need to worry about anyone seeing anything they shouldn't, unless there's things you don't want me to see, in which case you're out of luck. I see everything that happens around here."

"I bet." Theo chuckled, but the sound came out more nervous than anything.

"Okay, so since we're not going flying today, why don't you tell me a bit more about yourself?" James hoped to piece together a bit more about Theo. "A little woman at home? Nestlings?"

Theo rolled his eyes. "Nestlings? I don't know which branch of the shifting tree you fell out of, but all my family's been born human. And no, there's no little woman around…or man for that matter."

James laughed at the look on Theo's face. "Mine too. I was just throwing things out there. Haven't found anyone that catches your fancy?"

A soft sigh escaped Theo. "A few times, but nothing that really lasted. One of the problems with living among humans is finding people you can totally trust, and or finding other shifters."

"But you're from New Mexico, they used to have a big shifter community down there." James hoped he hadn't over played his hand. Theo hadn't said where he was from, but if he was involved in the human attack, he was from Santa Fe.

Theo gave him a sideways look. "If you're into wolves, which I'm not. They tend to be really cliquish and other than my family, I'm not big into groups. We're also a bit of a ways from a lot of shifters. They stick close to Albuquerque, even if they claim to control most of the state."

James patted Theo's leg again. So far, Theo hadn't made an attempt to move away from him. A long time had passed since he'd had another shifter sitting so close to him; particularly one as sexy as Theo. James really hoped his gut feelings were right and there was no way Theo was a killer. "I hear you there. So, if you were looking for someone to be in your life, what would you look for?"

"I don't know." Theo seemed to relax a little bit. "Another raptor shifter would be nice. I dated a raven for a little while, but he was just kinda…crazy…easily distracted"—Theo shrugged.—"I don't know how to describe him. But it just didn't work out right. I've only met a few other raptor shifters and most of them have either been taken or not my type."

"So you *do* have a type." James grinned. Theo *had* said him when referring to the raven, so obviously he liked men. "What do you look for in a guy?"

"I kinda know it when I see it. It's hard to pin down."

James sniffed and caught the distinctive smell of the potatoes getting done. The smell mingled nicely with the aroma of roasting hare. He stood and offered Theo a hand up. "Smells like dinner's about ready. Why don't we take this inside?"

Theo stood easily. "Okay. So what else can I do to help put the finishing touches on it?"

"I'll hand you some plates you can set out, unless you want to mash the potatoes." James didn't care either way. He stooped to pick up his sweats and paused to slip them on.

"Potatoes," Theo offered. "That way you can set the table the way you like it."

"Okay." James fought back another smile. His heart leaned toward liking Theo a lot. The novelty of having someone who wasn't super pushy and needed a bit of help from him was nice. If someone pinned him down about it, he'd have to say one of the things he missed the most while living out in the middle of nowhere was helping people. Helping people and his precognitive gifts were the reason he'd joined the Enforcers at such a young age. When he felt he'd stopped helping people as much and started hurting them instead, that was a big part of why he'd left. He'd lost the ability to trust his superiors and no longer believed they thought about the best interests of the shifters as a whole.

It didn't take him long to get the table set, and by then, Theo had the potatoes ready. James pulled out the roasted hare and quickly cut it up into serving-sized pieces. Minutes later they had everything on the table and were seated.

Before he dove into his food James bowed his head and said a silent thank you to the hare for its life.

Theo stared at him for a second. "You're Christian?"

James shook his head. "No, more Buddhist than anything. I was just thanking the spirit of the hare for its essence. If it weren't for that, we wouldn't be eating this right now."

"Oh." Theo looked thoughtful as he pulled his fork out of his mouth. "I never thought about doing that before. But then we don't do a lot of hunting. Unless you count the meat counter at Wal-Mart as hunting."

"No, I don't." James pursed his lips and shook his head. He wasn't sure he'd ever understand city shifters. "It's considered polite to give thanks whenever something has given its life so you may eat. I don't know if horse shifters give grass thanks for its loss, but I think we predators should always honor those that fall beneath our talons, or fangs in some cases."

"I guess it makes sense." Theo bowed his head for a second before he took another bite. "I'll have to explain honor and respect to my brother when I see him again. It might help him understand the meaning of life better."

"Honor and respect can help you understand a lot of things." James cut into the meat on his plate and watched the juices mingle with the pile of potatoes there. Theo was fairly rough around the edges, in his opinion. But he was beginning to like Theo. There was a lot he could teach him, if Theo stayed around long enough. He wished he knew more about how Theo felt about him, and how soon he'd go back to being alone in the woods.

Chapter Seven

SETTING THE fork down, Theo stretched with a happy sigh. His belly was full for the first time since he left home and he wanted nothing more than to curl up on the couch and watch a movie. James didn't even own a television, so that wasn't an option. What passed for downtime in the woods?

James sat there with his hands forming a steeple, elbows resting on the table. He alternated from watching Theo and staring at a spot on the wall. His plate had been empty for a while. Theo had a second helping where James declined.

"I'm glad you approve. And thanks for the help. It was…nice having someone lend a hand." James ran a hand through his satiny black hair.

A lump formed in Theo's throat as he watched each strand slide back in place. He fought the urge to reach out and touch it, and felt heat rise in his cheeks when his fingers twitched despite his effort. James didn't fall into any category that Theo had found himself attracted to, but he honestly didn't have a type. That fact lay evident in the extreme differences in the men he'd dated. Not just human versus shifter, but everything in between.

"I don't mind helping," Theo said. "If you'd like, I can do the dishes."

A smile barely formed on James' lips when a pinging sound came from the computer. James' eyes went wide and he was out of the chair in a swift motion that didn't even disturb his furniture. He bent over the keyboard and hit a few buttons before Theo could even react.

"What's wrong?" Theo stood, his chair scraping against the wood floor.

James cursed under his breath. "Poachers. I've set up some motion-sensor cameras around the edge of my property, because they come out here thinking no one will notice the animals they kill. I notice, and it's one of the few things I'll take action against anymore."

There was a quality to James' tone that hadn't been there before. Theo could practically feel the loathing rolling off of James as he glared at the screen.

Hitting a few more keys and staying fixated on the screen, James clenched his jaw until the muscles twitched. Theo swallowed, hoping he was never on the receiving end of the intensity boiling in front of him.

"So you don't own a TV, but you've got your whole property rigged for surveillance?" Theo laughed at his own joke, until James turned his gaze on him. The laugh died in his suddenly dry throat and Theo glanced away. "Sorry, I crack jokes when I'm nervous."

"Why would you be nervous? They're after big game, not you." James said.

He hadn't even thought about the men being after him. Could they be? Theo shook his head, reminding himself that even if *he* mistook Enforcers for poachers, surely James would know the difference. "Um, it's just that…what are you going to do?"

James stood and strode toward the door, stepping out of his sweats as he did so.

Theo barely suppressed a groan. His groin tightened and he was grateful that James wasn't paying too close attention.

"I don't expect you to come with me, but I have to get those people off my land." James flung open the door, took two running strides, and changed in midair. Cussing under his breath, Theo pushed out of his pants as he scrambled after James. If he got too much of a head start then Theo would never be able to catch up.

A flash of wings disappeared around one of the massive pines surrounding the cabin, proving Theo right. Slower than he would've liked, Theo changed and took flight. He pushed himself as hard as possible in the direction James had gone. Oddly, his wings still felt stiff, but he didn't take the time to ponder on the reason why. It just felt good to fly.

Theo took to the air above the tree tops. He had a better vantage there and spotted James weaving through the canopy. The straight path in front of Theo would allow the distance to be closed quickly. So he put on a burst of speed to catch up. Theo didn't care for being back in bird form just in time for danger, especially not knowing what James would do. He felt like he was right back in the situation with Fynn and just as useless.

Ahead of him, James dipped down into the branches below and Theo had to admire his agility. Bigger raptor usually relied on strength versus maneuverability.

When Theo flew over the area James had disappeared, he slowed down and had the distinct feeling James wasn't headed in the same direction anymore. A pull in his gut told him to go left, so he banked that way. He finally spotted the other eagle on a branch. The sudden calm gave Theo pause. What was he doing?

James flicked his wing out and hit a rope. A log released and fell toward the ground, and three men who Theo hadn't noticed were there. The one in front carrying a big rifle took the full blow of the log to the head and crumpled. The other two spun around, looking for a ground level assailant. They didn't find one, of course, and didn't even bother looking up.

One of them signaled to the other and they headed in separate directions. James followed, quietly cutting through the air like a true raptor. Theo silently trailed James and tried to keep him in sight between the dense branches.

When the two men with guns grew a fair distance from each other, James banked to the right and hit another rope. Instead of a log dropping from above, this one triggered a loop closing around the man's ankle. Dropping his gun with an alarmed cry, the poacher flipped upside down and hit a tree. He didn't move after that, just dangled.

The level of preparedness baffled Theo. He had to wonder if James had military training. Though he'd have to ask after the conflict was over, because he'd like to know how James managed the training without getting caught by the ever-present Enforcers. Theo's thoughts were interrupted by a gunshot ringing through the silent forest, followed by an eagle's cry. He realized that James had moved on while he lingered with questions.

The echo made a direction hard to pinpoint, so Theo headed back in the direction that the other guy went. Another shot fired. Theo's heart threatened to explode with how fast it beat. He banked left and then right. James flew past him before he saw the last poacher. The barrel of his gun was lifted and following James' path through the trees. Something inside of Theo snapped. He hadn't been there to stop the man who attacked his brother. But he wouldn't let that be true for James.

That was the last coherent thought he had before his bare human feet hit the ground and he flat out ran at the man trying to kill James. With an inhuman scream tearing out of his throat Theo tackled the poacher. The gun went flying and all of the air rushed from the man's chest in a burst. Theo swung before the other man could regain his bearings. Wild punches hit the man's face as he choked for breath with wide eyes. The anger burning inside of Theo wouldn't let him stop. Some part of him acknowledged that this wasn't normal for him. That the look on the man's face should've been enough to make him hesitate. He couldn't get past the anger. Couldn't accept that someone else he cared about was in danger. He had to get rid of the danger.

"Theo stop! You'll kill him!" James appeared to Theo's right and caught his arm before he could land another punch.

"No! He deserves this for trying to kill you!" Theo tried to pull away, but James had an iron grip on his arm.

"Yes, he tried to shoot me, but you know it takes more than that to kill one of our kind. He's unconscious. Look at him!" Without letting go, James pointed to the man who hadn't tried to rise.

Theo looked down and could barely recognize the face of the poacher as being that of a human. Puffy purple tissue and blood covered every inch and made the features blur together. With a gasp Theo scrambled away. James let him go just in time for Theo to turn and vomit.

Thoughts raged in his mind, adding to the nausea. He'd done that. He'd disfigured someone. He'd almost killed a man. And James had barely been able to stop him. He wasn't a violent person, he wasn't. He knew he wasn't, but…

"Usually I'd call the rangers and have them come take these guys away. This time I think I should take them over by the highway and leave them. Hopefully someone will stop for them right away and get this one to the hospital. If I called the rangers, the poachers could press charges for assault, and probably win." James stopped at that, like the truth bothered him.

Theo wiped his mouth and turned back to face James. "How can I help?"

"Help? You've done quite enough. Get back to the cabin, I know you can find it. I'll deal with you when I'm done." James bent to lift the poacher.

"Wait, but I was just—"

"I know what you thought you were doing. Go now. I can't even look at you." James proved that statement by turning on his heel and walking away.

Theo put a hand on his chest where his heart clenched painfully. All he'd wanted was to protect the man he loved. Pain lanced through his chest as the realization dawned on him, bringing Theo to his knees in the now empty clearing.

Hours passed before James returned to the cabin. It took a few tries for Theo to find it, partially because he couldn't change right away and had walked aimlessly in the dark, but also because he couldn't see through the tears. When he did finally change, it was very simple to find the cabin. Then he felt compelled to clean up after their meal. Only a short time before they'd sat at the table, enjoying good food and better company.

He'd just got a fire blazing in the wood burning stove when James walked in, clad in pants for once. Theo shot to his feet from sitting in front of the warmth. He shivered at the look on James' face, steely like cold metal and sapping the newly created heat from the room.

"I told you I didn't want to know what happened to you before and why you showed up here, injured and unwilling to shift. But what I saw today makes me think I can't trust you. What were you thinking?" James closed the door behind him, cutting off the cool night air he brought with him.

"I don't know, I—"

"You don't know? How am I supposed to believe that?" James pressed his fingers to his temples.

"It's not like that!" Theo tried to form the words in his brain.

"No? Then what *is* it like? What, you haven't had enough time to make up a good story? Some sad sob bit that just proves you're misunderstood?" He crossed his arms and squared off with Theo.

The posturing didn't help Theo to straighten things out and he stuttered for a moment.

"That's what I thought. You need to leave. I can't have you here. Be glad I don't call the Enforcers. Someone who can attack another living being for no reason has no honor." James stepped back and motioned towards the front door.

"It wasn't for *no reason*. Can't you see that?" Theo couldn't sort his emotions any better than he could his words.

James hesitated, clenching his fists at his sides. "I know what I saw," James said, though his words were soft.

Theo closed the distance between them in one step and gripped James by the shoulders. "But you don't know me well enough to know what I felt."

"I don't need to. You're violent. A danger to our kind." James took a half step back and glanced down, as if he couldn't quite accept what he said. His chin brushed over top of Theo's hand, staying there for a moment before he shook his head and tried to turn away.

Seizing the opportunity of that hesitation, Theo grabbed James by the back of the neck and kissed him as hard and as deeply as he could. He let out a strangled cry that Theo smothered. James put his hands against Theo's chest and tried to push. Again, not with true conviction. Theo had a guess of how strong he was. If he really wanted to push him away, James would have Theo pinned on the floor. The thought made Theo groan and he deepened the kiss, happy to feel the last of James' resistance slip as he slid his hands around Theo's waist.

Theo pulled away and smiled at the heavy-lidded expression on James' face. "I couldn't control myself today. I don't even know when I decided to shift. All I knew was that that man was shooting at you and I had to stop him. You were all I could think of."

James' lips parted, like he wanted to say something. Instead he placed a gentle kiss on Theo's mouth. Groaning and shaking, Theo closed his eyes and savored the taste. James pulled a hand back and cupped Theo through the sweat pants. His length had hardened during the kiss and Theo hissed against James' mouth at the contact.

"I haven't had a man in a very long time." James said, staring at Theo's lips like he wanted to devour them more. He slipped his hand inside of Theo's pants and wrapped his fingers around the bulbous tip of Theo's cock.

Theo gasped and slid his hands down to cup James' ass. With one fluid motion, Theo picked James up while James began to stroke Theo's length. He carried him toward the bedroom and kicked the door fully open. James moved his body with the rhythm of his strokes, grinding their hips together like Theo was a pole for him to dance on. When they reached the bed James jumped down, kicked out of his pants, and knelt on the mattress. He kissed Theo again, and then moved to kissing his way down Theo's neck to his chest. He swirled a tongue around one taught nipple, making Theo groan, and then moved to the other. Theo gripped James' shoulders and tried to watch through the haze of sensation flooding him. James kissed down past Theo's navel and closed his lips around the throbbing tip of Theo's cock. Theo gasped. He'd only ever had this once. Usually he was the one giving.

"Mmm, you taste salty." James practically purred.

James swirled his tongue in circles before taking as much of Theo's length as he could. Theo grabbed the back of James' head and thrust his hips in time with James' bobbing. His cock swelled and he worried that he'd cum way too soon. He slowed his motions, moaning openly when James took the cue and slowed his sucking to long, torturous pulls. With one last hard suck on Theo's cock, James turned around on the bed, backed up, and bent his head down.

"I want you to fill me now," James said.

Theo's tip still throbbed and pre-cum leaked from the tiny opening. He took the moisture and rubbed it over the whole tip and part of his shaft. Then he pressed his tip to the opening of James' tight ass. Theo pushed forward slowly, gripping James' hips and pulling him back at the same time. James moaned and then cried out when Theo filled him completely.

"Gods of the Sky!" James looked back at Theo over his shoulder, panting. "Fast or slow. I don't care. Just. Give me. All of it."

Happy to oblige, Theo thrust his hips and drew another cry out of James. He started a slower rhythm, making sure James had time to adjust before he sped up. The pressure built in his balls, it had been too long since the last time, and Theo panted with the need to cum. He focused on James and that helped. Each groan, each moan, and every curse James let out, Theo took note and moved so that he hit those spots multiple times.

"I'm going to cum. Are you close?" Theo didn't want it to be over yet.

"You first. I'll follow," James gasped.

Thrusting his hips as hard as he could, Theo pushed himself over the edge and let go. "Fuck!" The release shook him to his core. Every muscle in his body shook and his knees almost gave out. His body locked up and he had to stop.

"No. I'm so close. I need more." The plea came out as little more than a whimper.

Theo pulled out with cum still oozing from his cock and flipped James over on his back. Lifting James' legs over his shoulders and pushing James further up on the bed, Theo swallowed all of James' dick down to the tight balls. It twitched in his mouth and he began sucking as hard as he could. James gripped fistfuls of the quilt beneath him. Theo dug his fingers into the muscles of James' ass, encouraging his hips to move with him as he bobbed his head. James' must've been close, because in moments he cried out and exploded in Theo's mouth. Theo drank him down, every drop, until James lay quivering on the bed, completely spent.

Chapter Eight

THE SOUND of soft snoring jarred James awake. As sleep fled him, it took him a moment to remember Theo was in bed with him. He wasn't sure how to react, and simply lay there for a time while accepting the presence of a man in his bed. Rolling over slowly, he studied Theo in the morning light coming in through the curtains. Theo was still a mystery even if the memory of their sex the night before was exciting. James had wanted Theo gone, and at first the kissing had felt like a diversion, but then they'd both surrendered to it and it felt wonderful. But with the sunlight chasing the shadows away, he was back to wanting to get to the core of Theo. There were still too many questions, but he had to find a way to ask them and not let Theo distract him.

Theo rolled over. He looked young in sleep even with dark stubble covering his jaw line. But he wasn't the first man James had been with who looked younger in sleep than awake. The look also lent an air of innocence to him, something that hadn't been present the previous evening when Theo had tried to kill the poacher. If Theo had really been defending him, James could almost understand the reaction. It also showed that somewhere in Theo's past, he'd failed to defend someone else. Rage like he'd seen didn't just spring up out of nowhere. There was something, or someone behind it. Unfortunately, it also could've surfaced before, and been aimed at a human while Theo was in eagle form. If the latter was the case, then James had slept with a sociopath. Filing that thought away for another time, James ran a hand gently up the meaty bicep closest to him and trailed his fingers over Theo's chest.

The brown skin there was free of scratches. The shifting he'd done had obviously finished the healing process. But it still didn't answer the question of what had caused the scratches in the first place. There were more and more questions that needed answers, and James worried they might somehow fit into the case of the eagle attacking the human in Santa Fe.

James sighed. But if that had been the case, why hadn't Theo stayed in bird form when he attacked the poacher? None of it made any sense. There was something missing, something major.

As gently as possible, James leaned over and kissed Theo's stubbly cheek before he slipped out of bed and went to greet the morning. He hoped a round of exercises would help clear his head and let him think straight. Laying there looking at Theo only served to muddle his brain even more. Even before the sex, he'd felt drawn to Theo. After sex it was stronger than ever.

James slowly lowered himself back to the ground, and then raised his arms above his head. The exercise had become simple over the years, but still managed to energize him.

"You do that every day?" Theo asked from behind him, near the cabin.

Without lowering his arms, James looked back over his shoulder at the handsome man standing on the porch. "Most days. Every now and then life gets busy and I don't get it done."

Theo sat on the edge of the porch. He once again had on just a pair of sweats. James really needed to go into Billings and get Theo something more to wear.

"No incense today?"

James moved his arms out so they were parallel to his body. "I didn't want to wake you with the smell. That's also why I came out here. It's another nice day."

Theo leaned back and smiled. "Yeah, it is. What are we going to do today?"

James put his hands on the ground and lifted himself up into a handstand. Even upside down, Theo still looked great. "I was thinking about heading into Billings to pick you up some clothing that might actually fit."

"Might not be a bad idea. Can I come?"

"It might be a little hard to explain you wandering around in just a pair of sweats until we get you a shirt." James grinned and lowered himself back to the grass. "Not to mention, my sweats are just a bit tight on you."

"There is that." Theo looked thoughtful for a moment. "I could always just hang in the car."

Laughing, James stood. "Car? Do you see a car around here? You really are a city shifter."

"How do you bring supplies in? You can't hunt for everything you eat. Even a sack of potatoes is more than we can easily carry in flight." Theo scratched his head. "Besides, what's in the shed over there?" He pointed to the large shed just inside the tree line.

"Snow mobile. In the winter I'd rather not hike back in if I can help it. So when I go after things that are more than I can lift in bird form, I take the snow mobile." James walked to the porch and sat next to Theo. "I fly to town with a backpack rolled up in my talons. After I get what I need, I hike back out here. Takes most of a day."

Theo looked surprised. "You were planning on taking all day and leaving me here alone?"

James shook his head. No matter what connections he formed with Theo, he was reluctant to leave him at the cabin unsupervised for too long. "Nope. I just wasn't planning on getting that much in the way of clothes, a couple of T-shirts and a couple pairs of sweats and some deck shoes. I can fit it all into a single canvas bag and still be able to carry it. Not a big thing."

"Sounds like you've done this before."

"Yeah. I find injured eagle shifters in the forest all the time. Sometimes I swear it's like they fly all the way out here to just drop from exhaustion so I'll fix them roast rabbit."

Theo laughed. The sound was very pleasant and James found himself hoping he could hear more of it. The idea of listening to Theo laugh made him realize that with Theo around, winters wouldn't be so cold. "You make some pretty awesome rabbit."

"It's probably because it's fresher than what you'd catch at *Wal-mart*." James grinned.

"Wait a minute." Theo frowned. "Now you're making fun of me for being a city boy."

The look was more adorable than James could resist. He pulled Theo close and kissed him. Theo's lips were sweet and a soft sigh escaped him as their kiss lingered. James could've sat there on the porch kissing Theo all day, but that wasn't resolving any of the questions going through his head.

"I don't know if there's any sport in that, it would be too easy," James said as their lips parted. "I doubt there's much honor in it. I'll try to resist."

Theo stood and took a couple of steps away from the porch before putting his hands on his hips and glaring at James. "See that you do. It's not my fault my family wasn't the outdoorsy type and like having neighbors around." He relaxed and crossed his arms. It made his biceps bulge a bit and James flashed back to those strong arms around him the previous night. "But I have to admit, I might be able to get used to being out here. It's relaxing."

"That it is." James stood and wrapped his arms around Theo. "Will you answer a couple of questions for me?"

Theo swallowed. "If I can." His body went tight even as he returned James' hug.

"Did you attack that man in Santa Fe?"

A heavy sigh escaped Theo. "No."

With Theo in his arms, James didn't need any extra powers to tell he wasn't lying. But he also knew Theo hadn't told the whole truth either. "Do you know who did?"

Theo looked away. "I'd rather not say."

James touched Theo's chin and turned his face so he could see Theo's eyes. "You realize that's a yes.

You were trying to protect someone and failed. That's why you went after that poacher so forcefully. You didn't want to fail again."

"Yes." Theo closed his eyes and a shudder passed through his body. "I had to do something to protect you. You've done so much for me. More than anyone beyond family ever has. I didn't want you to get hurt." A tear trickled down his face, rapidly running toward his stubble. "You don't even really know me."

"But I'd like to." James kept his voice just above a whisper and briefly kissed Theo's quivering lips.

Theo hugged James tighter. "I want to know more about you, too."

James didn't like making Theo cry. He wanted answers, but he was over the anger he'd felt the previous night. If it was the feelings surging through him for Theo, or something else, he couldn't tell. He only knew he wanted to make Theo happy. That simple need was suddenly very important to him. In his years as an Enforcer, he'd never found anyone he wanted to make happy. Since disappearing into the mountains, James hadn't had the opportunity to even try. The only other shifter in the area was a bobcat, and felines rarely dated avians. And vice versa. For a moment James lingered on how and why Theo had crashed into the forest and broken his wing, but he decided not to worry about it yet. Maybe the fates were trying to tell him something.

"Okay." James stroked Theo's hair. It was thick and rough, different from his own silky locks even if the color was similar. "Tell you what, let's fly into town and get what we need. I can use a few things beyond just clothes for you. I think the hike back will be good for you. We can talk more on the way back."

Theo straightened and looked at James. "So, you'll let me fly to town with you?"

"That's what I just said. But we are going to talk more on the way home. It's a nice long hike. Not overly hard, but long." He gave Theo another quick kiss. "Now, let's get cleaned up. I don't know about you, but after last night, I need a shower."

A wide grin spread across Theo's handsome face. "I wouldn't say no, especially if we can share the hot water."

James took Theo's hand and led him back onto the porch. "If we take too long, we'll be out after dark. It's not a huge problem. Most of the predators around here know me and give me a wide berth, but since we're not owls or wolves and the moon is not that bright right now, it'll slow us down a bit."

A wicked gleam illuminated Theo's brown eyes. "And what could I do to slow down our shower?"

"Oh, I bet you'll think of something." James pinched Theo's left nipple. Rolling the soft flesh between his thumb and forefinger until it got hard. "Besides if we take too long we'll run out of hot water. That's not a huge thing to me--"

Theo chuckled. "But as the city shifter, it'll be a little irritating to *me*. As long as you're there to keep we warm in the cold deluge, I might be able to survive."

As far as answers go, Theo's wasn't bad. James laughed, feeling even more at ease with Theo than he had before. Even knowing Theo knew something about the Santa Fe attack, James let himself relax. Being with someone felt good, and for the first time in a very long time, he let himself simply enjoy another person. He promised himself he wouldn't get mad at whatever Theo had to say, and they'd find a way to work out what had happened to send Theo flying so far from home.

Chapter Nine

RUBBING THE washcloth across his wet body, Theo glanced over his shoulder at James, and not for the first time since the hot spray started. He tried to behave, he really did, but when James bent over to grab something off the rim of the tub, Theo landed a well-aimed smack to the proffered bare ass.

"Hey now, that's precisely the time-consuming behavior I was talking about." James didn't jump at the contact, but kept lathering instead.

The smile Theo hadn't been able to get rid of since the night before got wider. "I can't help it, you presented me with too great a temptation."

James cocked an eyebrow at Theo as he stood up. "As do you, but we won't get anything done if we give in now."

"Would that be so bad?" Theo moved to encircle James with his arms.

"No, no." James placed a wet, soapy hand on Theo's chest. "Just turn around so I can wash your back, you horny man."

Pouting with lips he'd used many times to get his way, Theo slowly turned around.

"Any other day I would offer to bite that bottom lip. Nice try, but we're still going." James took the coarse washcloth and soaped up Theo's back.

He had to admire James' dedication. When the man put his mind to something, he stuck to it like glue. Theo closed his eyes and savored the warmth he got from being cared for.

James added his hand, effectively massaging the tense muscles. Theo groaned and placed his palms on the tiled wall in front of him.

"James? I don't think that's helping our cause." Theo hated himself for saying it, but another part of him really wanted to show James he could be responsible.

A deep sigh left James' lips and tickled Theo's back. "I know, you're right. This was more difficult than I expected."

His scalp prickled as relief loosened the tension in his jaw. Theo had felt certain his treacherous cock, and its tendency to stand at attention every time James touched him, would make him appear to be no more than a hound dog. That fact made warmth spread throughout Theo's body. "I'm all clean. I can get out if that'll help."

Theo waited for a response, but none came. He turned to find James staring off at nothing in particular. James shook his head, as if bringing himself out of deep thought. He glanced at Theo and nodded.

"That would probably be for the best," James said. "Especially with that temptation." His eyes locked on the engorged length of Theo's cock. He reached out, as if to touch Theo, then snatched back his hand and swallowed hard.

With a nod, Theo wiped his face and slunk out of the shower to get a towel. He dried himself off and tried not to think about James anymore than he already was. Luckily for his kind, shifting worked as well as a cold shower.

James seemed distracted while he finished some things before they left. He wouldn't look directly at Theo. When Theo mentioned it, standing on the porch in naught but his skin, James tried to brush it off with a wave of his hand.

"It's nothing, honestly. I just get a bit jittery before going into town." He too wore nothing but his skin. "Are you ready?"

Theo nodded, still not sure if James was being evasive or not.

They stepped outside and James shifted first. He picked up the rolled canvas bag he laid on the porch earlier, took to the air, and landed on a tree branch close to the cabin. Theo followed suit, picking up his own rolled bag with his talons and taking off in the direction James flew as he launched from the branch.

The journey to Billings took a while. James kept their path over trees and away from the road. Theo had no comparison to say whether or not that added extra time to the trip, he was simply grateful that his wings carried him the whole way. After the flight from Santa Fe he hadn't been sure about longer trips any time soon.

Billings was nowhere near as far as Santa Fe, but relief still filled Theo when they landed close to the tree line just outside of town. Theo stashed his bag behind a tree and shifted while he had cover. He slipped on the sweats he'd brought and then motioned for James to do the same. Theo scanned the surrounding area to be sure they didn't have an audience while James returned to human form and got dressed.

"Alright, I'll go get you some better fitting clothes so you can go with me to the general store. Stay out of sight, okay? We don't want any unnecessary attention." James peeked around the tree, then stepped back and placed a light kiss on Theo's lips. "I'll be back soon."

"I hope so." Theo mumbled as James sped off through the field. He crossed his arms, not because he was cold from the lack of shirt, but because he felt on edge letting James leave his sight. James obviously knew what he was doing, but Theo felt like he was being watched as he stood there under the trees. Maybe it was because he happened to be the wild card in this situation. Aside from being born in Arizona, Theo had never left New Mexico before. They all moved to Santa Fe when he was nine and his brother was about to be born. His mother never told him why, but he assumed it had something to do with the dad he never knew.He would never have considered Montana as a destination. Maybe upstate New York or Oregon. He read somewhere that Oregon was really nice. Fate, it seemed, had other plans.

A family walked down the road, holding the hands of their two kids and laughing at some inside joke. The mother had a brilliant smile and the father couldn't take his eyes off of her. The interaction brought with it a pang of guilt. Theo hadn't stopped to worry about his family in the past couple of days. He wondered when it would be safe to try to contact them, so he could make sure they were safe.

James appeared around the corner about fifteen feet behind the family. His head was down and acted like he didn't even take note of the people walking with their children. In fact, he made it all the way back to Theo without really looking up.

"Okay, I got a couple of pairs of longer sweats, two loose fit tee's, and some slip-on deck shoes. Like we agreed. Does that work for you?" James finally looked up, his brow furrowing. "What?"

Theo shook his head. "It's nothing, I'm just missing my family is all. Hey, are you okay? You seemed even more distracted than before."

"I'm fine, I promise. Let's go get what we need from the general store and we can head back. The sooner the better." James handed him the bag of clothes. "Put whatever you don't use in the canvas sack."

Rather than argue, Theo did as James asked. He had to admit, it felt so much better wearing clothes more his size, even if he still went commando. The cotton was a little more scratchy than James' beat up old pair, and he missed the feeling of intimacy from wearing another man's clothing.

"Much better fit. And I like the way the shirt covers your chest. You have my stamp of approval, let's go!" James marched off back toward the buildings.

Theo shoved his extra clothes in the canvas sack as he followed.

Billings was more urban than Theo expected. He'd been imagining an old-time town with more horses than cars, but it was actually no different than most of the cities in New Mexico. Though Santa Fe could be described as bigger. The "general store" that James spoke of turned out to be a local grocer that carried some extra odds and ends as well. Theo smiled at the misuse of descriptors.

A bell jingled overhead when the door opened. It was a nice change from the normal mechanical ding of other stores. The smell of fresh fruits and vegetables hung heavy in the air. James smiled and waved to the older gentleman behind the counter.

"Hey Burt. Need some of my usual. Get your shipment in yet?" James continued walking as he spoke.

"Sure did." Burt nodded, his gaze drifting to Theo. Under the gray brush of the man's beard, thin lips set in a hard line.

Trying to smile and be pleasant, Theo moved his gaze to where James stood, shuffling through potatoes. A shiver rode down Theo's back as he passed the counter, but he didn't show it outwardly.

"Um, can I help grab something?" Theo said.

"Sure. I was thinking about grabbing some carrots for stew. There's a few herbs I need to restock on, but I'll grab those. Anything you want to get?" James had a knack for multitasking.

Theo would've laughed, maybe even made some snarky remark, but the store clerk set him on edge. Instead he picked up a plastic baggie and picked out some fat carrots to put inside. "Would it be alright to grab some green chilies? I saw you had eggs in the fridge. My mom showed me how to make a mean huevos rancheros."

"That sounds great. Grab whatever you need. Just remember that we have to carry everything back to the cabin." As if that reminded himself, James dusted his hands off and moved away from the potatoes.

The carrots would be more than enough for stew. Theo tied the bag and grabbed a few more to fill with the ingredients he needed. The feeling of foreboding he got from the clerk intensified, so Theo rushed through the rest of his shopping. He found James in the herb isle, just finishing up with a small baggie of something green.

"Did you by chance grab some cilantro?" Theo ran a finger over one of the shelves filled with containers.

"No, but you can grab some." James smiled and then pouted his thin lips. "You need to stop making that face, it worries me."

"Sorry," Theo said, looking around and lowering his voice. "That clerk gives me the creeps."

"Who, Burt? Don't mind him. He's a shifter too, a bobcat. Maybe that's why he gives off a vibe." James touched Theo's arm, spreading warmth with the contact.

"That's probably it then." Theo didn't know much about bobcats. The predators he was accustomed to were werewolves.

James seemed perfectly fine. No doubt or fear, he continued to smile like it was the most normal thing in the world. "Shall we head back? If we leave now, we should make it back just after nightfall."

"And we can talk." Theo said it more to himself, but James nodded.

"That too."

They checked out at the counter with a debit card that James pulled out of a small pocket in his canvas bag. Theo kept his gaze averted from Burt, hoping it would lessen the tension. At least he tried. Only when they walked out and made it a block away from the store did the feeling finally leave him.

"So where would you like to start?" Theo wanted to get the ball rolling as quickly as possible.

"Okay, down to business." James adjusted the straps of the bag on his back. "Well, I know you don't want to tell me about who is behind the attack in Santa Fe, but I need to know if you're in trouble with the Enforcers."

Regretting being proactive, Theo considered how to handle the whammy dropped right out of the starting gate. "Technically? Yes."

"Technically?"

"Well, I mean, I didn't do anything wrong. Except taking responsibility for a mistake that shouldn't have happened. That I shouldn't have allowed to happen." Theo hated how he had to struggle to find the right words. He desperately wanted to say the right thing, the honest thing, and not upset James again.

James sighed heavily as they passed into the tree line. "Okay, that goes back to the person you're protecting. But there's more to it. Enforcers are judge, jury, and executioner when the need arises. If they're hunting you, I need to be aware so that I can take measures."

He could only guess what measures James referred to. "I'm pretty sure they're looking for me."

"Alright, that's a step forward. Did one of them follow you here?"

"Not all the way. I lost them in a lightning storm, in northern Colorado."

"Is the lightning what hurt you?" James climbed over a fallen log and offered Theo a hand to follow.

Theo gripped the proffered hand, grateful for the contact, but too soon he had to let go. "No. The falcon had some kind of energy attack. Since I was in a storm, I equated it to a ball of lightning. He managed to hit me with one."

"That's why you were in such bad shape." James sounded more thoughtful than accusatory. "You probably only managed to stay in the air because of your golden eagle blood."

"I think I acknowledged that on some level, even then. But I didn't have time to see what happened to the falcon. I hope nothing bad."

"Yes, I hope so as well."

They fell into a comfortable silence for some time as they walked. Theo hadn't been on a hike for quite some time. The forest was beautiful and the light of the sinking sun played through the dense branches of the trees. Theo stepped closer to James and entwined their fingers. Where their hands touched sent tingles through Theo's skin.

"We're not too far now. We've already passed onto my property," James said.

Evening set in as they walked, and Theo smiled in response. "You sure do know your stuff out here. Though I have to admit, I thought you'd have more questions."

"I was enjoying having someone to hold hands with. You've painted a pretty good picture for me. I'll wait until you're more comfortable talking to me for the rest of the story."

"Which may be sooner than you think," a female's voice rang out, strong and clear.

James grabbed Theo and stepped in front of him, turning to face the direction the voice originated from. "Show yourself. You're on private property and I'm not afraid to use force."

"Oh, Mr. Chan, I wouldn't dream of engaging *you* in combat." A tall red-haired woman stepped out of the shadows wearing all black. Her skin was pale and flawless, and her long hair was pulled back in a ponytail. But her brilliant green eyes practically glowed in the dim light, giving her an eerie and somewhat cold feeling.

"Then what *do* you plan on engaging in, if I might ask?" James didn't step away from Theo and put his hand up when the woman took another step.

"My name is Naya and I'm a truth seeker for the elite Enforcers. I'm here to get the truth out of one Theo Montoya involving the death of a fellow Enforcer."

Chapter Ten

JAMES STARED from Naya to Theo and back. "The death of an Enforcer?" His heart sank. After the talk he and Theo had while walking home, and the connection they seemed to be making, he struggled with the new information thrown in his face.

Naya nodded slowly. "Sylvester Comstock, falcon shifter assigned to northern New Mexico since the raven twins were reassigned to south Texas. I believe you helped train him."

Leaning up against a nearby tree didn't help the sudden spinning in James' head. Sylvester had been his final trainee in fact. A strong man with a good conscience. Even when Theo had mentioned a falcon shifter throwing energy balls, James hadn't made the connection. His training with Sylvester had been in basic Enforcer protocol, not the use of his special gifts. The last James had seen of Sylvester had been in New York, as he'd handed him over to an owl shifter with a similar talent to finish out his training before he was assigned a territory. "Sylvester, my gods."

"Wait a minute," Theo sounded indignant. "You're an Enforcer?"

James shook his head, trying to think straight. "No, not anymore." He looked up and glared at Naya. "I left the Enforcers years ago."

"We thought you were dead." Naya cocked her head. "You did a pretty impressive job faking that, didn't you?"

"I had to. I couldn't deal with what our superiors demanded of me." James pursed his lips. "But this isn't about me, this is about Theo."

"You are correct, although I'll need to update the Enforcers' files on you to correct extraneous information. There may even be an inquiry."

"Fine." James rolled his eyes. If he needed to, he could vanish again. Disappearing wasn't hard in the Rocky Mountains. He might even go and live as an eagle for a little while, although he'd miss the few friends, like Burt, he'd made in Montana, it was better than getting under the thumb of the Enforcers again. "You said you're a truth seeker, so you have that gift?"

Theo continued to gawk at the two of them. "What gift? Oh, wait a second, is this like those energy balls the falcon was throwing at me?"

James looked at Theo. For a moment he had the urge to incapacitate Naya and disappear with Theo into the forest. "Yes, it's like the energy balls. Some Enforcers have special gifts--"

"Mr. Chan!" Naya objected. "You were sworn to keep the existence and details of the elite Enforcers a secret."

James spun back toward her. He'd lost all patience with the Enforcers and their rules years ago. "I'm no longer an Enforcer. The oaths I swore then don't matter now. I'm still dead as far as the Enforcers are concerned, at least until you tell them otherwise." He looked back at Theo. "As I was saying, some Enforcers have special gifts that let them do their jobs a little easier. Truth seeking is a psychic talent that lets the wielder know when the truth is spoken. She's like a living lie detector."

"Oh." A thoughtful look appeared on Theo's face. "Do you have any special talents?"

With Naya standing right there, hands on her hips and a dangerous glare in her eye; James knew he couldn't lie without her calling him on it. "I can get flashes of the future. It's not an active talent and I haven't had a flash in years."

Theo's brow furrowed like he wanted to argue. "That's not how you found me?"

"No." James took Theo's hands. "I don't know what it was that led me to you, but it wasn't my gifts. But I *am* thankful I found you."

Before he said anything, Theo swallowed hard. "I am too."

"Look, can we please get on with this?" Naya interrupted. "I'd like to get my investigation closed as soon as possible."

James resisted snapping at her. For a moment he wondered if he'd been so pushy and arrogant when he'd been an Enforcer. He turned Theo's hands loose and stood at his side. "Okay, fine, ask your questions."

Theo blinked. "Wait, right here? In the forest? Shouldn't we go back to the cabin?"

"Here is fine." Naya craned her neck slightly. "Theo Montoya, did you kill Sylvester Comstock, the falcon who pursued you from New Mexico?"

"No." Theo squeezed James' hand.

"Did you engage him in combat?" Naya continued.

"I defended myself when he came after me, but I didn't attack him first."

"Did you see him fall?"

"We were in a storm cloud," The first definitive sounds of nervousness came through Theo's voice. "There was lightning all around. He was throwing those balls of energy at me. Then he stopped. I didn't know what happened to him."

Naya cocked an eyebrow. "That's not entirely accurate, but not entirely a lie either. Please, try again."

Theo seemed to deflate in on himself and squeezed James' hand harder. "The last I saw of him he was spinning out of control. Falling. I couldn't get to him. My wing was hurt, because he managed to hit me with an energy ball. It was all I could do to stay aloft. If the winds hadn't been so strong, I would've hit the ground. I didn't know he died."

"That is the truth." Naya sighed. "This is more complex than I had anticipated. Did you attack the human in Santa Fe?"

"No." The word came out as little more than a whisper.

James wished he could take Theo in his arms and lend him strength. He'd been under a truth seeker's scrutiny back in Enforcer training. He knew it was uncomfortable, particularly when they were probing for questions you didn't want to answer. All he could do was hold Theo's hand and silently reassure him it would be okay.

"Do you know who did?" Naya continued to prod.

"Yes." The word came out harder than the previous one.

"Tell me."

Theo glared at Naya. "My brother," he spat out. "Are you satisfied? My brother Fynn did it. He tried to go for a flight without me, and there was some human that came out of the trees and attacked him. I was covering for him, he's only fourteen and it makes no sense what the guy was even doing there in the first place. But that's what family is supposed to do, take care of each other." His hand in James' shook.

Naya nodded slightly. "That's what I needed from you. Unfortunately we still have three situations to deal with."

"Three?" Theo looked from Naya to James. "What's she talking about?"

James sighed. He knew what she was getting at and it was going to make things difficult. "You fought with an Enforcer. As far as shifter law goes, that's very similar to resisting arrest in the human world."

"And is not to be tolerated," Naya added. "Now, I believe, is a good time to retreat to the cabin over the ridge so we can sit down and further our discussion. We also need to discuss the human hunters who were found alongside the road not far from here. They were fairly roughed up."

"But alive," James said. "It's my right to defend my property. I've been doing it for years."

Naya gestured for them to start walking toward the cabin. "It is, but we still need to talk about it."

For a moment, James thought about defying her and just sitting in the forest and finishing their discussion there, but the weight of the pack on his back reminded him he had some groceries he wanted to get put away. He nodded at Theo as a sign they should go along. They traversed the short distance to the cabin in silence.

James did his best to act like Naya wasn't invading his territory. They sat down at the table once he had his supplies stashed and Theo returned from the bedroom after putting the new clothes away.

While they'd been working Naya had her phone out, sending messages or playing games. James wasn't sure which and didn't really care.

"Okay, if you're done, can we continue now?" Naya asked after they were all seated.

"Sure," James said. "About the poachers…they weren't hunters. Hunters have proper licenses and do things during the correct season. The men we intercepted were poachers."

She nodded at him. "I do understand the distinction between the two. But all three of them had major injuries. The local authorities report this as a common thing. They get an anonymous call and then find poachers in need of medical attention along the road. It doesn't really bother them because it means someone is doing their job for them. I will give you points for making sure to leave evidence of the crimes with the people you catch, but Mr. Chan, you risk drawing attention to this part of the forest and thus to you."

James laughed. He had heard a lot of local legends since he'd moved into the area. Even before he'd started his campaign against the poachers, the locals said his land was haunted, or had a vicious family of Bigfoot living on it. He hadn't done anything beyond making sure the legends continued. "I doubt the locals really care. This land has been the source of various legends over the years. If you check the local records, you'll find they go back over a hundred years. I'm not doing anything but defending what is mine. If you really investigate, you won't find a single mention of a flying man, or a vicious eagle attack in the area."

"I'll do that." Naya continued. "But I do suggest that if you insist on attacking people like this, that you at least start spreading them out along the road to make it look less like it's happening on your property and more like it's happening elsewhere."

Even though James could see the logic in her request, her general air of superiority grated on his nerves. "And what about you letting the Enforcers know about me?"

"Already done." She set her phone on the table. "There will be a tribunal about you faking your death. The elite Enforcers are trying to decide who'll be on it and how soon they can arrive."

James cocked an eyebrow. "Arrive? They're coming here?"

"Of course. It's been a very long time since we've had to judge one of our own. The other Enforcers want a chance to hear your side of things." Naya shook her head and tapped a long, well-manicured nail on the table. "They believe this is too important to leave to one Enforcer."

"That's a lot to convey through the texts you've been sending." Theo glared at her.

James made an effort to lighten his expression. Theo gave hard enough looks for both of them. "There is a special code Enforcers can use between each other to convey a lot of information in as few key strokes as possible," he explained. "Texting was just getting popular when I felt the need to vanish. I never really got the hang of it."

Naya sighed. "Again, you're revealing too much. You should be more careful with your words, Mr. Chan. Even if Mr. Montoya is your mate, and you haven't indicated that he might be, there are certain things you keep between other Enforcers."

For a second, it felt like Naya slapped him. James blinked as his brain bubbled in turmoil. Could Theo be his mate? Strange energy had been flowing around them from the start, and it made sense for a bond to have led James to find Theo in the forest. He wished he knew for certain.

"James." Theo touched his arm. "What's wrong? You look like you've seen a ghost."

"No." James shook his head, pushing aside the idea that he and Theo might be at the start of their mating process. "Just remembering something."

Naya frowned, obviously having detected the lie, but for some reason didn't call him on it. "Anyway, Mr. Chan, before I leave I'll set a binding around your property to prevent you from leaving until the tribunal arrives. It shouldn't be more than a day or two at most. Being able to move quickly is why all Enforcers are bird shifters."

Theo laughed. "And now who's letting out secret information? Most people don't know that. We just hear Enforcers and our knees get all wobbly and we want to run for the hills."

"Mr. Montoya, I suggest you hold your excitement," Naya asserted. "Unlike with Mr. Chan, I get to decide what happens to *you*. Unfortunately, I don't believe we can do that here in Montana. I will need to interview your brother and the rest of your family before your fate is decided. It is very valiant of you to want to protect your brother after he attacked a human, but in your attempt to do so, an Enforcer lost his life. There will be consequences."

James shook his head. "And you think you're going to haul him out of here and force him back to New Mexico? You already know he didn't attack the human and he was just defending himself from Sylvester."

"And as a former Enforcer, you know how we feel about people defending themselves against us. We are the law for the shifters. Without us, it would turn into chaos very quickly. In most cases we're the only ones who stand between the shifters and the humans. Mr. Montoya fought an Enforcer. Even if he didn't attack the human, and had good reasons for claiming he did, it doesn't balance out the fact that Sylvester is dead."

"I understand about the loss of Sylvester." James could still see the young Enforcer full of excitement and ready to do everything he could to keep shifters safe. Years ago, he would've been standing at Naya's side ready to haul Theo in, but that was before he became disillusioned by the Enforcers and their way of doing things. "But we…you…need to determine if it was an accident or not. You need to judge the man Theo is, and not just the act he was part of. Even Enforcers aren't above the law. We don't know if

Sylvester was using excessive force. He was throwing energy balls at an innocent man. Theo should've been detained for questioning."

"Who at the time we all thought was guilty, due to actions he took on his own to perpetuate the situation," Naya countered. "He's answered my questions honestly. I sense he has a good heart. That's the only reason he's still alive at this point. If I get the answers I need from his brother and mother, he may continue in that state. If not, then we'll have a problem and I may be forced to eliminate his entire family."

Theo's eyes went wide. "What?"

James' heart sank as he flashed back to the reason he'd left the Enforcers. He wanted to do everything he could to help Theo. But beyond making things worse by attacking Naya and flying as far away as they could, the only thing he could think to do was wait for his tribunal. He had to hope the members who showed up would be willing to see some level of logic for both him and Theo.

Chapter Eleven

THEO KEPT his face as calm as possible. Inside he felt like he was lost on a roiling sea. So many questions battled to be answered. Why would his whole family have to die, for any reason? How could the Enforcers, who were meant to protect the shifter community, arbitrarily decide to end lives on a whim? Why did James keep the fact he was a former Enforcer a secret? Could he be Theo's mate? Why hadn't his mother ever explained to him about mates before? Was that why his father left them? Because his mother wasn't his father's mate? And why did that man have to attack Fynn in the first place? None of those questions would matter if his brother hadn't been attacked. Then again, he never would've met James. Thoughts battled emotions inside of him and he wasn't sure how he kept from screaming in frustration.

Naya sat back in her chair and crossed her arms. "I'll wait for confirmation from my superiors about the tribunal before I take Mr. Montoya back to Santa Fe."

"But once it's done, once they've decided what to do, you can come find me. Right, James?" Theo managed to keep his voice from trembling, but only just.

The muscle in James' jaw twitched several times as his eyes narrowed. "Come find you? In Santa Fe? Leave my home… unprotected?"

Even without the distinct panic Theo picked up in his voice, he knew what it would mean for James to leave his land to the mercy of poachers. Still he had to ask. "Well, yeah. Don't you want to be with me when they decide my family's fate?"

"Yes, of course I do, but…" James looked Theo in the eyes and left the unspoken words hanging between them.

Theo wasn't catching something. "But you won't come for me? Is that it?"

James just sat there, unblinking.

"As much as I hate to interrupt this, is there any way I can use your computer, Mr. Chan?" Naya said.

James glanced at her with a tight-lipped expression. Theo thought he'd snap at her again and tell her to butt out of his privacy. Then James' expression changed and he looked away with a curt nod.

"Thank you. I'll be quick." She stood in a graceful way reminiscent of how James moved.

Once she was engrossed in whatever site she pulled up, Theo leaned in and whispered to James. "I don't understand. If we're mates, and whatever that means, why won't you come for me?"

The tone of James' skin paled. "It's a bit hard to explain right now, but I just can't. Not just because of poachers. I worked really hard to escape this kind of life. I don't even know how I'm going to handle the people I used to work with, let alone if I'm capable of taking on the role of mate. You can either accept that fact or not."

Theo's heart clenched. Pain sliced through him like he'd never known. Everything James said made sense. His concerns, his fear, and his hesitation. But it didn't stop Theo from feeling like it was his fault, like he wasn't good enough for James and *that* was the real reason James didn't want to leave his mountain paradise. Hell, he wouldn't want to leave this place if it was his home either.

With a nod, Theo sat back again. He turned his attention to the woman whose fingers were flying over the keyboard. His skin heated as he sat there, excessively aware that James watched him, but also too nervous to say what his heart screamed. To tell him everything. That he loved him. That he couldn't face the next two days without him. That he never wanted to be without James ever again. He dashed those thoughts away, knowing how selfish each one sounded.

Eventually Naya stood up. "All right, I've made sure all the information I've accessed has been erased. No harm will come to your system. I have clearance to take Mr. Montoya as soon as we can be ready to leave. The tribunal will be here by tomorrow evening. They're chartering a private plane into Billings."

"And how exactly will *we* be traveling?" Theo asked before James could open his mouth.

She cocked an eyebrow. "By our own propulsion, of course."

"Flying in bird form? Won't that take longer?" Apparently the tribunal rated a jet, but they didn't. Theo tried not to feel snubbed, anymore than he already did.

"Not exactly. With having to purchase tickets on a flight leaving today, getting through check in, and avoiding security, it would keep things much simpler to just use our gift of bird form." Naya spoke as if she were stating the obvious. She even said it a little slower, like she spoke to a child. Naya had no problem making it known that she valued shifter law above all else, and that she saw their abilities as a blessing from a higher power.

Theo didn't feel like the combination left much room for his innocence. He turned to look at James, who wore a blank expression. "Are you going to be okay? I don't want to leave you to deal with this all alone."

"You don't have a choice in the matter. We have interviews to execute." Naya interjected.

Theo wrinkled his brow at her words, but didn't take his gaze from James' face. "Talk to me, please."

The please part finally got a reaction and James looked up into Theo's eyes. "She's right, we don't have a choice. I must stay and face my superiors, and you have to go prove this was all self-defense."

"They aren't your superiors anymore." Theo took James' hands and squeezed them."If you asked me to, I'd stay, and neither the devil nor my mama could pull me away."

James opened his mouth several times. His gaze shifted to Naya a couple of times before he could manage a response. "Whether I work for them or not, they still have the power to take our lives if they decide we've broken the law. I can't be responsible for any harm befalling you. Please, go with Naya and get this mess cleared up."

Theo released their clasped hands and instead cupped James' cheeks, getting close enough to feel the heat of his breath. "Then promise me you'll come down to Santa Fe as soon as you can, as soon as this tribunal thing is over with."

"He won't know—" Naya began.

"Please shut up." Theo bit out in a soft tone. He almost closed his eyes at the sensation of touching James, but didn't want to break eye contact.

"I don't think I can, Theo. I haven't left this area in many years. It's not just my home, but my sanctuary." James seemed breathless as he spoke the words.

His throat tightened as he said the next words. "James, what if I never see you again?"

Under Theo's hands James twitched, his face creasing in what had to be pain. "Please don't say that."

"But it could happen. All of this could end badly. And you and I would never even know about it, until it's too late." Slowly Theo pulled away.

Grabbing Theo's retreating hand, James shook his head. "I can't think about that right now, it makes my head hurt. I have to believe we'll see each other again. Fate wouldn't be so cruel as to bring us together just to tear us apart like this." His voice cracked ever so slightly.

"Um, I'm truly sorry, but we really need to go. Mr. Montoya, we have a deadline. Forty-eight hours in which I have to reach a decision." Naya was more hesitant this time. "If I fail to come to a judgment by then, another Enforcer will, and they might not care about the truth at that point."

Perhaps a truth-seeking Enforcer *could* have a shred of decency, in spite of her tendency to trample other boundaries. Theo looked down at James' narrow fingers wrapped around his wrist. "I hope you're right, James. I really do."

James swallowed hard and Theo couldn't help but watch his throat work. He really wanted to kiss James, to tell him that of course they'd see each other again, but the pain in Theo's heart wouldn't let him. He refused to beg for love. From anyone.

With one last, longing look at James, Theo got up from the table and walked toward the door. He swept his arm out in a gesture for Naya to precede him. "After you."

Naya looked back at James, almost as if she wanted his permission, and walked with a stiff gait toward the door.

"Theo…" The plea was soft, barely audible even.

Theo almost immediately turned, he wanted to see James' face one more time, but couldn't manage to do more than pause.

"Be safe, for me." James breathed the words like a prayer.

A sigh left Theo and he followed Naya out the door. She was folding her clothes into a knapsack, completely undeterred by her current nudity. With a shrug Theo began to undress as well, setting the clothes on the wooden barrel by the door. He would have clothes once he got home.

"So, since I didn't ask before, what kind of bird are you?" Theo scratched his head, not wanting to be the first one to shift.

She shot him a crooked smile over her shoulder and bent into her shift. When the process was done, an impeccably white swan flapped her wings. Even to Theo she was one of the most beautiful things he'd ever seen. He smiled wryly at the thought of flying home in such elegant company.

Chapter Twelve

JAMES STOOD on his porch and watched Naya and Theo fly away. Naya paused and hovered for a moment, a surprising feat for a swan. Energy poured out of her, locking him in on his own land. Frowning, he sat on the edge of the porch and stared at the ever-darkening sky until he couldn't see Theo anymore. He swallowed, put his elbows on his knees and his head in his hands.

His heart hurt. Even though he'd only known Theo a couple of days, there was no denying a bond had formed between them. He'd been trying to decide what was going on, and when Naya suggested they might be mate bonding, he immediately wanted to deny it. Deep inside he knew she was right. Finding a mate was something he'd nearly given up on. But if he was completely honest with himself, he hadn't been looking for a mate. After everything the Enforcers put him through, finding a person he'd be driven to defend above all else wasn't a high priority. The encounters with Theo had been brief and intense. He couldn't deny he was drawn to Theo, more than anyone he'd met before.

But that fact might not matter since the Enforcers were back in his life. Naya led Theo toward Santa Fe and potential doom. James sat on his porch as the night creatures continued their cycle of life and death, even as his world fell apart in ways he'd never dreamed possible a week earlier. The ache in his chest increased with each passing moment, knowing the distance between him and Theo grew with each painful beat of his heart.

James hopped off the porch and stomped out into the middle of the clearing in front of the cabin. Exercise normally helped him clear his head. He started with simple stretches. His body welcomed the familiar movements. For a few minutes, he focused on gestures and actions he'd done on reflex for years. Everything went as it should, then he lowered himself to the ground and lifted himself up with his arms. When he started to balance on one hand, he wobbled and crashed to the ground.

After four more tries, he finally gave up and walked back into the cabin. Even the separation from his family had never interfered with his exercises. The inability to focus showed him exactly how much Theo impacted him. The last time he'd been unable to balance had been the time he'd been told to kill his own family. What happened then had been wrong and the mess Theo was wrapped up in was wrong, too. James pondered how to work through the situation as he stared at the contents of his fridge. He couldn't find a way out of it for either of them, nor could he force food to be appealing. That was what had him so off balance. Not the food thing, but the fact that they were both facing possible death and he couldn't find a way out of it.

Turning on a single light, James waited for the computer to boot. He didn't feel like having more than one light on, it felt too fake. The world was grim and he craved real light. Unfortunately, the only real light he'd found in his life currently flew toward an unknown fate. James wanted to talk to someone about it, but his old channels were no longer open. Even the few people who still knew he was alive wouldn't be able to help him out of this kind of mess. He was tempted to try and find a way through the spell Naya had set around his land, but he felt sure Naya wasn't a fledgling and wouldn't leave a weak point for him to exploit. Enforcer magic wasn't so fragile. That's why they'd formed the elite branch in the first place. His own gifts weren't the sort to get past what Naya cast. The tribunal, on the other hand, *would* have the ability to bring down the barrier.

The first thing James noticed when he got online was a bulletin for a missing shifter. A golden eagle shifter in Albuquerque was missing. James stared at the emergency post. It was too close to Santa Fe not to be connected, but the missing shifter was a woman. From the picture posted she was Caucasian, not Hispanic. He didn't see how it could be related to what Theo and his brother were going through.

James's world tilted. He grabbed his head and struggled to focus. For the first time since he left the Enforcers, his gift flared to life. Something was happening, or would be happening. Colors swirled behind his closed eyes and he felt a tug, like someone had a rope around his middle and used it to pull him forward. The sharp scent of metal filled his nose. He opened his eyes and tried not to breathe in the reek.

The comfortable surroundings of his cabin were gone, replaced instead by an ugly gray-scape.

A cold room that left James shivering.

Eagles lay scattered and covered in blood.

Their flight feathers were missing, leaving gaps in their spread wings reminiscent of missing teeth in a smile.

Tubes ran from bruised arms without even the courtesy of a bed to lie on as they were drained.

Blood dripped onto a concrete floor, making it clear the insertion hadn't been done by a professional.

Wolves howled in the distance. Somewhere nearby a coyote yipped. A mountain cast a long shadow as the sun grew higher in the sky outside, visible through the solitary window.

When James looked back from the window, Theo lay on the floor in place of the others. He looked trapped between his two forms. Feathers spotted his brown skin in odd rows that didn't make any sense. Pain etched deep lines in his handsome face as he stretched toward the only other person in the room. A teenager who looked like Theo lay on the concrete floor, covered in blood and feathers.

No!

It took all James' training and focus to pull himself out of the vision. The tie connecting him to the future snapped and left him feeling like he'd jumped from a plane without a parachute. The metallic tang of blood still clung to the back of his throat even as his cabin living room spun back into stark relief. He sat panting for a moment and then stumbled to the kitchen sink to splash water over his face.

James dashed from his cabin into the cool Montana night, throwing his clothes off as he ran. Shifting before his pants hit the ground, he flew into the darkness. The shield Naya put in place around him shimmered brightly, as if in warning, but he didn't pay it any mind.

James hit it at full force. Light blazed up around him. Blinding him. He tried to stay in the air, but he couldn't tell up from down. He careened out of control for several heartbeats. Bark brushed against his feathers. Panic set in and he flapped his wings in a wild attempt to avoid a collision. The ground turned out to be a lot closer than he expected. He hit hard. Specks of light filled his vision, both from the flare of magic and the impact. He tried to blink the spots away, but could only flop on the ground and managed a pathetic squawk.

He was truly and completely trapped. Something awful was about to happen to Theo and he had no way of escaping his prison. The irony wasn't lost on him. He couldn't even call to warn them.

James shifted back to human and put his head in his hands and wept. He couldn't remember the last time he'd cried, but the despair welling up inside him was worse than anything in his life. His heart cried out to be with Theo and he couldn't, even though he knew beyond any doubt Theo's life was truly in danger. There was nothing he could do about it until after the Enforcer Tribunal passed their judgment. He could only hope Naya could keep Theo safe, and wasn't part of the vision of blood.

Chapter Thirteen

THE FLIGHT back home was a lot less dire than the one before. No lightning clouds. No Enforcer chasing Theo and shooting balls of energy at him. No accidental death. Instead, Naya flew beside him with the grace and calm of her natural counterpart. She flapped her wings more than he did, but the power of her flight remained undiminished. Swans were built for distance, just like eagles were built for hunting.

In spite of her tendency to spout rules and advice, Theo kind of wished he could talk to her. The miles would go by so much faster and be slightly less dull. Since he didn't have talking as a distraction, and nothing to gaze upon but the open stretches of Wyoming, all Theo could do was think about James.

At first he replayed their time together in the bedroom. When he found that line of thought made him physically uncomfortable, he shuffled through all of things left unspoken. Something bad had happened to James, he knew that for sure. Naya probably knew what exactly. But what could have him so terrified that he refused to leave the cabin? And what of the suggestion that they were mates? Was James rejecting him? Thoughts of his mother being left to care for two sons alone swam in his mind. If the mate bond was such a sacred thing, how could anyone reject it in the first place?

Theo swerved around a small flock of birds they spooked as they passed a stand of trees. Some part of his mind, the autopilot perhaps, acknowledged that they passed into Colorado. They were close to the area where the falcon fell. It may have even passed by already, but not even the grim thought could force his mind away from James.

His heart clenched and he lost his breath. The edges of his vision blurred and he glided toward the ground without making a conscious decision. He managed to maneuver into a small stand of trees as he landed, but didn't spare the time to look around before he shifted back to human form.

A thump of heavy wings signaled Naya's arrival. Theo couldn't look up. Everything spun as he knelt on all fours and wondered if he would heave or pass out.

"What are you doing? We are way too exposed here and could be seen. The road is less than a mile away…" She trailed off and then she was there, brushing his hair away from his face. "What's wrong? You're very pale."

He pressed one hand to his chest and tried to slow both his breathing and his pulse.

The soft skin of her palm brushed against Theo's sweat-soaked brow. "You've broken out in a cold sweat. Take deep breaths in through your mouth and out through your nose. That should help."

Still unable to form words, he did as she asked, taking several deep inhalations and closing his eyes.

When he opened them, the fog on his vision lessened and the spinning reduced to a slight tilt.

"Any better?" She asked, adjusting the nap sack still slung over her back.

He nodded. "I'm sorry, I have no idea what happened. I was thinking about James and everything went all wonky."

No response came, so he looked up. Naya's lips were pursed as she stared off at nothing. He mopped his brow with the back of his hand and sat heavily on the ground.

"Penny for your thoughts?" He aimed to lighten the tension that seemed to have settled out of nowhere.

Naya glanced at him and then down at her hands. "Just thinking about an unforeseen complication. If you and Mr. Chan began your bond, but hadn't quite completed the connection, then it'll be quite uncomfortable for the two of you to be apart. I made the mistake of assuming that you two hadn't bonded yet."

"How do you know that? Are you bonded to someone?" Theo didn't like to pry, but she seemed so sure of her assessment.

"No." She said, almost under her breath. "I have studied all the source material available to the Enforcers and have spent some time with groups of different species of shifters. There are many subtle and not so subtle differences between them, but one constant is how the bonding affects those involved."

Theo shook his head, trying to muddle through the analytical delivery of her words. "What would make you assume that James and I hadn't bonded yet?"

"Because he let you go." The lack of hesitation to her answer was like a slap to the face.

For a moment, the spinning threatened to return and claim him. He fought it back for a silent stretch of time.

"If not for the urgency of the situation, I would return you to Montana. I may not have a bond myself, but I understand the theory of it. But we must get you back to New Mexico, find your family, and decide your final judgment." She placed a hand on his shoulder. "Please. Can you manage the rest of the trip?"

He wanted to say no. He wanted to scream to the heavens that he had to get back to James and tell the stubborn man they were meant to be together. The thought of James' continued rejection kept him from doing just that. Having the man he loved abandon him again would be asking for a punishment worse than death. "Yes, I can make it."

She smiled and helped Theo get to his feet. Then, after a thorough investigation of the area while he waited in the trees, Naya deemed the area secure enough to shift back to bird form. Once they were back in the air, Theo focused on his family and seeing them again to stave off the overwhelming crushing sensation in his chest. Distance only seemed to increase the pressure, but his resolve warred against it with each passing mile.

Santa Fe seemed almost like an alien landscape, even though he hadn't been gone for long. The trip took its toll in exhaustion, but couldn't compare to his flight north to Montana. Theo wished he could look upon his home with the reckless abandon that he had before. Too much had changed. *He* had changed.

Naya hung back and let Theo take the lead. The last leg of the journey stretched out, almost as if he walked the streets below. Finally, they passed over the park of clustered trailers he called home with his mother and brother. He came in to land in the wooded area where he and Fynn went to shift for their flights. The same place where Fynn was attacked, because Theo had been late that night.

Landing with a flutter of kicked-up debris, Theo quickly hopped out of the way so there would be room for Naya. Once she folded her wings to her side, he shifted and went looking for the bag of clothes he kept hidden in a shallow hole under a fallen log. There were just some thrift store shoes, pants, and shirts that would fit both him and Fynn. Theo half expected everything to have changed in his absence, so he breathed a sigh of relief when he found the bag exactly where he left it.

Naya already pulled her clothes from the knapsack. She moved with the same calm grace as before, but her gaze never seemed to stay on any one thing for long. Theo hurried to pull his clothes on. Not because he worried about Naya seeing him, again, but because he needed to feel his arms around his mother. That was the only thing that would sooth the ache radiating from his chest and threatening to consume him the moment he let his walls down.

"Will it alarm your family to explain who I am?" Naya asked as she pulled her shirt down.

Theo thought about it for a moment while he tied the laces of his shoes. "I'm gonna say no, seeing as how

I've been gone for a bit. The fact that I'm back will probably be more important to them. I just hope my little brother is home."

She nodded. "That is a concern we share. I would prefer to interview them consecutively."

A laugh bubbled up Theo's throat. "You speak so clinically some times. Does it help with having to pass judgment on people that could end their lives?"

"Sometimes. But the taking of a life should never become an emotionless act. No matter what, even if they're the most evil being ever encountered, I never forget that I'm extinguishing an existence from the world." She motioned in the direction of the mobile home park. "Shall we?"

Theo nodded. She seemed pretty sure of her position in the matter, but he guessed she'd have to be in her line of work. He offered the Enforcer a slight smile, as if she could hear his thoughts, and stepped through the trees.

The light above the front door was on, but there were no sounds coming from inside. He knew his mom would be home from work, and he expected to at least hear the radio going if not the TV. A chill caused goose flesh to rise over his arms and back. Theo swallowed and turned the knob on the door.

Soft light filled the empty living room. To the right, down the hall, the doors to his bedroom, his brother's room, and the bathroom were all dark. Back to the left, the living room and kitchen sat in a quiet stasis. Usually the dishwasher would be going, food cooking, or at the least a neighbor sitting at the table sharing daily news about the park. The small hall leading back to his mother's room also lay in shadow, but at least had a slight glow at the end.

"Mamá!" he called down the hall.

Something tipped over, followed immediately by a curse in Spanish and a door slamming open.

"Fynn? Fynn, is that you?" His mother's tone held all the warmth and love of home, even if she sounded extremely annoyed. She rounded the corner with her brow scrunched and lips pressed in a thin line, until she saw Theo.

"Hi, Mamá." He smiled and held his arms open.

She hesitated, glancing back and forth between Theo and, he assumed, Naya behind him. Then she rushed forward. Just as Theo wrapped his arms around her shoulders, a stream of prayers came out of his mother's mouth. He flinched as her prayers turned into more cussing and she slapped at his arm.

"What in the world were you thinking trying to take the blame for your idiot brother? He needs to learn his own lessons! How dare you leave and not tell me! And your work's been calling. I had to tell them you were sick. I've lost all control over my sons, and I can't even think straight at work! I won't even mention the mix up I almost made with the pool chemicals. Why didn't you call me? You're in so much trouble, mister!" The red in her face drained slightly as she panted for breath.

"I'm--" he started.

"No! Then you come home with some woman! And I know damn well she's not your girlfriend, so start explaining!" She set her fists to her hips in the familiar sign that she was ready to hear what he had to say for himself.

"I'm sorry Mamá, I didn't mean to worry you. It's really important that we all sit down with this nice Enforcer and have a talk. Hopefully that'll answer all your questions. But we need Fynn. Do you know where he is?" Theo knew a couple of places his brother liked to be. He could track him down if he needed to. The sooner they got everything sorted out the better.

The look that crossed his mother's beloved face banished all other thoughts. Tears welled up in her eyes and Theo stepped forward to wrap his arms around her.

"What's wrong?" he asked.

Even with her shorter height, she gripped his shoulders and mumbled against his chest. "That's why you should've called. I've been going crazy here without you." A sob shook her. "Your brother wanted to help you, he felt guilty, so he—"

She stopped long enough that Theo held her back at arm's length. "What? What did he do?"

Large teardrops fell freely down her cheeks to splash unnoticed on her t-shirt. "He went to the wolf pack in Albuquerque to ask for help. I haven't heard from him since."

Chapter Fourteen

JAMES' COMPUTER beeped, alerting him to someone entering his property. He brought up the screen with the camera on it. There were three people, two men and a woman walking calmly down the main path toward his cabin. Even through the fuzzy video he recognized the smaller of the two men. Short, chunky, but all muscle, Orville Jones hadn't changed much in the years James had been hiding in Montana. The great horned owl shifter was easily one of the most powerful Enforcers, and James's stomach knotted in anger at him being there. He wondered if Orville'd been able to assume control of the group. James presumed that at least one of the three was the current leader; it didn't make much sense for them to send three people who were just flunkies to talk to him. And potentially kill him.

He'd been thinking about it since Naya and Theo flew off. He couldn't recall ever hearing of an Enforcer leaving the fold, especially from the elite class. They were a tight-knit group and becoming one of the shifter lawmen was a lifetime assignment. If word got out to the shifter community that he'd slipped away from them, even made them assume he was dead, it would tarnish the Enforcers' reputation. Keeping the peace wouldn't be an assured thing anymore. For those reasons, it wouldn't take much for the Enforcers to just kill him if they didn't like his answers. He hadn't wanted Theo to see that, so no matter how much his body ached with the separation between them, he had to stay on his toes. They were both going to need to be very strong if they were going to survive their encounters and find a way to get back together.

"James Chan!" Orville's deep voice bellowed from outside the cabin.

James stood and walked to the door. He took a deep breath and squared his shoulders before he stepped outside. "Orville Jones, it's been a long time."

The woman with him, a tall elegant woman with the start of gray in her hair and heavy laugh lines, who, if James was going to guess, had to be some sort of crane or heron, gasped. "So Naya was correct. You are still alive. I had hoped she was mistaken and it was someone pretending to be you."

"No." James closed his door and walked to the edge of his porch. "It's really me."

"And you know why we're here," Orville said.

"Of course." James sat down on the top step and stared at the three standing a few feet away. He wanted to get the upper hand quickly and figured throwing them off guard was a good way to do that.

"You don't seem overly worried," said the other man. He was an average looking man with long brown hair and a sharp nose, most likely a raptor of some kind.

James shrugged. "I learned a long time ago that the Enforcers are going to do what the Enforcers are going to do. All I can do is present my case and hope you'll see things my way." With Orville there, he doubted that would happen. Orville hadn't been real open minded in the past, and James figured he hadn't changed much over time. He didn't know anything about the other two, or what he would need to do to sway them in his favor. He just hoped he could do it fast enough to make it to Santa Fe before his vision of Theo came to pass.

"Ever the Buddhist, aren't you, James?" Orville said.

"It's worked for me so far," James replied. "So where do you all want to start? I guess you're all dying to know why I faked my death and came out here to live in the middle of no-where."

Orville glanced around like he wanted somewhere to sit. James didn't want them in his house. It'd been hard enough having Naya in there. If they wanted to sit, they could either take a seat on the porch with him, or in the grass. He doubted they'd do that because it would put him on the high perch, and birds hated not having the high perch.

"Let's start with introductions," the woman said softly. "You already know Orville, and if he'd been minding his manners, and had a proper sense of decorum, he would've started with that. I'm Eluna Simmons, Enforcer stationed in the Florida panhandle." She bowed slightly to him. "Next to Orville is Paul Reid from Washington DC. With Orville, we are a third of the current Enforcer Council of North America. We are here to hear what it was that drove you to leave our numbers and seek solace here in the northern wilderness."

James returned her bow. "Thank you, Ms. Simmons." He inclined his head to Paul. "Mr. Reid."

Eluna pulled a tablet computer from the bag she had slung over her shoulder. She tapped it several times. "Now, Mr. Chan, our records show that you disappeared nearly five years ago. A body of an eagle was found near the site of your last assignment, which was left incomplete. It showed signs of being torn apart by talons. There wasn't much left, but it did have your Enforcer brand on its left foot, which is why it was assumed it was you."

With pursed lips, James nodded. "That's correct. It wasn't easy to do, and took a little planning, but I branded a oneform eagle who was my size and then tore him to shreds, making sure to leave the talon with the brand so you would think it was me." He didn't add that it had been one of the hardest things he'd ever done and he'd spent months afterwards cleansing himself and asking the spirit of the eagle for forgiveness. Now that he'd been found, the eagle's death seemed too high a price for such a short reprieve.

"That was a rather extreme measure to take," Reid said solemnly as he put his hands behind his back and stared at James. "Why go to all that trouble?"

James made an effort to hold his temper. If he planned to get out of Naya's enclosure around his property and save Theo, he had to get through to the shifters before him. "What do your files say about the nature of my final assignment?"

Eluna looked at her tablet. "You were to eliminate a family of shifters who'd become too friendly with some humans and were risking exposing the community at large." She frowned. "That's odd, the details are missing. I don't have any names on this file."

Tense anger shot through James. His feet flexed and he had to stop them from shifting to talons and ripping up the step they rested on. He took a slow calming breath. "Orville, do you remember what I was sent to do? You were the one who gave me the assignment."

Orville paced around. "You were to kill your family. I had people in place to kill you after you completed the job."

"What?" Some of Eluna's demeanor slipped. "Orville, we have never been so cruel as to request agents kill their own families. Another agent should've been sent. We need to see the evidence against them."

James couldn't stand it anymore. He stood and walked to the bottom of the steps. "Yeah, Orville. We'd like to see the evidence against my family. Why did you want them killed? We weren't socializing with humans. There was no risk. I was a good Enforcer. I was slotted to be one of the greatest."

Orville scowled. "Is that what your precognition told you? That you were destined to be one of the greats? Maybe you were. You were rising in the ranks quickly enough."

A cold realization washed over James. He desperately wanted to wrap his hands around Orville's neck and snap it, leaving him flopping around on the ground until he died. "You set me up. You're the head of the Enforcer Council now. You were worried I'd get elected in a few years and you wouldn't. My family had never done anything wrong. It was all about you."

"You can't prove that." Orville scoffed. "You're a disgraced Enforcer, come back from the dead. I'm the head of the council, you said it yourself. I earned my rank with hard work and dedication."

James shook his head and paced away from them. He wanted to go into the cabin and slam the door, but he had no idea what their powers might be…well, he knew Orville could control the weather. Beyond that, he didn't know with the other two. They might be able to burn down the cabin around his ears. "Look, as much as I want to rip you into a pile of feathers right now, I don't have time for that. There are other, more important things for me to do. I need to put the past behind me. I honestly thought I had. I've kept my head down for five years. I never told anyone what you'd done to me and my family. I've never even contacted my family. As far as they know I'm dead. But I need to go save my future. We can deal with my past later."

"What do you mean?" Eluna asked.

"Naya has taken a young golden eagle back to investigate an eagle attack on a human in Santa Fe." James focused his words on her. Deep inside he felt like his best chance of getting through to one of them lay with her, Orville would never see his side, but a tribunal let all the attending members have a vote. If he could get Eluna on his side, maybe Reid would vote with her and he could fly free. "Moments after they left here, I had a vision. The wolf pack that rules most of New Mexico is draining eagle shifters of their blood. Theo and his brother were among the bodies. If I hurry, I can get to them in time." Cold gripped him at the thought of actually leaving.

Eluna nodded. "I received a report from Naya right before we landed in Billings. She reported that Fynn

Montoya was missing when they arrived in Santa Fe. She is accompanying Theo Montoya in his search for his brother. They were in route to Albuquerque to confront them."

James' heart sank. Even if he managed to catch the leading edge of a storm front and fly with all his might, he might not be able to reach them in time.

"Orville, I think there is more to this issue that we need to investigate," Reid said. "It will take time to call the whole council together to review the situation. I vote we hold off on passing judgment until we can discuss it with everyone. Mr. Chan, we will need you with us at that time."

"That is a very suitable solution, Paul," Eluna bowed again. "I shall inform the other members of the council we need to convene as soon as possible. Until that time, I shall keep Mr. Chan in my care. Orville, stay with Paul. If you should fail to show up at the council meeting, we will find you."

Orville turned a brilliant shade of red. "I'm not the one who's disgraced the Enforcers and faked his own death! You make it sound like I'm the one on trial here."

Eluna smiled. "That's for the council to decide." She unfastened the shoulders of her dress and let it drop to the ground. "Now, Mr. Chan, we need to take a short flight to the airfield. Unlike Orville and Paul, I have my own personal aircraft, as soon as we arrive, we'll be in the air and heading to save your mate."

"I don't know for sure he's my mate." James objected, but was quickly pulling off his sweats and shirt. He couldn't deny there was a good chance he and

Theo had started bonding. It would explain the emptiness in his gut after Theo and Naya flew away.

"You're desperate to save him, I can see that, and it was in Naya's report. Now, please follow me." Her form blurred and a tall, elegant sandhill crane stood in her place. She slipped her head through the strap of her bag and took to the air.

James shifted, grabbed his clothes in his talons and followed her. As he neared the trees, he heard Orville and Reid shouting at each other, but he didn't care. He had a reprieve and had to do everything he could to save Theo.

Chapter Fifteen

CONVINCING HIS mother to stay home proved more difficult than Theo would've liked to admit.

"Why should I stay?" His mother blocked the door with fists bunched on her hips.

Theo felt a swell of aggravation. On any other day, he'd appreciate the concern. On any other day. "I can't have you in danger. One is enough!"

A hard line set on her rounded face as she looked up at her son. "I will tear down the world with my bare hands to protect my boys!"

"Ms. Montoya, please. I completely sympathize with the need to protect your sons, but arguing is wasting valuable time, and Theo and I can travel much faster if we fly."

If Theo hadn't been paying such close attention, he would've missed the twitch in the tense muscles of his mother's face when Naya hit a nerve. To her credit, Mariposa Montoya managed to reduce her temper to a stream of Spanish cursing as she stepped aside. Theo had only witnessed such an occasion once before in his whole life. He and Fynn always went out of their way not to remind her she was only human. She was great at dealing with human things, but shifter life was often more than she could handle.

"You just be sure to bring back both of your hides intact, yours and your brother's. So I can tan them myself!" His mother slammed the door after their exit.

Theo couldn't hide the half-smile he wore as they headed back to the place they'd landed. Even though he knew it was a sore subject for his mother, the fact that she was human made him appreciate her in a way he didn't think he could if she'd been a shifter.

"I'm not sure if I can see where humor is an appropriate response to any of the current circumstances," Naya said from beside Theo.

As ever, she spoke the truth, but Theo still laughed. "I know I shouldn't find it funny at all, but seeing my mother speechless before launching into curses is a rare thing. Thank you, by the way, for convincing her to stay behind."

Naya seemed to consider his words for a few steps. "You're most welcome. As much as it would be more expedient for her to be on site when we locate your brother, the potential for danger is too great to justify the risk. And what I stated about time being crucial is quite accurate."

"I couldn't agree more." Theo began to disrobe as soon as they were out of sight of possible onlookers. "But she never would've listened if it'd been just me trying to convince her."

Naya simply nodded in response and then pulled her shirt over her head. Theo knew she had a pleasing figure, by anyone's standards, but felt grateful her nudity didn't bother him. At the same time, he could tell his naked form didn't bother her either, and her gaze seemed to assess him the same way she'd assess a tree. After they bundled their clothes for flight, Naya began to shift a few heartbeats before Theo, and took flight as soon as her form settled. Theo followed suit and matched the steady pace Naya set in the direction of Albuquerque.

Theo used the time they were in bird form to work out a game plan. He didn't know many people outside of Santa Fe, but there was a shifter he'd gone to school with who had moved south a couple of years back. Rats and any kind of raptor usually didn't get along for obvious reasons, even though they both came from traditional Hispanic families, he and Benny remained pretty good friends. Benny tried to get Theo to move, or at the least come visit, on a regular basis. Theo was usually too busy.

Come to think of it, Benny owed Theo. Benny had gotten cornered by some kids in school, kids wanting to do some not-so-nice things to the rather large rat they'd found. Theo had risked himself, not to mention shifters at large, by haphazardly shifting between two buildings and swooping in to snatch the scared rat before the boys could snag him. Theo never had a reason to cash in the favor before, but maybe Benny could repay him by helping track down the wolf pack. Rat shifters generally knew the under belly of whatever city they lived in. Perks of the species as it were.

The landscape below rolled by, riddled with hills and rocks, and interspersed with the rough vegetation that thrived in arid conditions. Theo never noticed the difference until he'd been exposed to the lush green of Montana. And he never thought he'd miss a place so much with only being there for a few days. The ache in his chest told him it wasn't just the scenery he missed, but he couldn't let himself be drawn into a line of thinking which would distract him from the task at hand. There would be time for worrying about James later, when his brother was safely home.

The gleam of Albuquerque finally came into view. Theo heaved the avian equivalent of a sigh and brushed his wing tips against Naya's to get her attention. She gave a soft trumpet before making a slow descent toward the ground. They finally touched down a mile or so out of the city. Theo dropped his clothing several feet before landing so as not to get tangled when he landed. Naya had her knapsack strung over her back.

When they were both back in human form and fully clothed, Naya rubbed her hands up and down her arms. Theo didn't feel cold, but he didn't know what kind of circulation issues a swan might have.

"I should message the Enforcer for this area. He should know I'm following leads in his territory." She fished her phone out of the nap-sack and slung it back over her shoulder.

"Yeah, I need to get a hold of Benny, a friend from school. He's a rat shifter and might be able to help us find the wolf pack." Theo watched Naya's face, expecting her to have some kind of reaction to his declaration. Instead she simply looked up from her phone and nodded.

They both made their perspective phone calls, Theo waiting to use Naya's phone since he'd forgotten to grab his from his room. Luckily the number he needed was simple enough to remember without access to his contacts. Benny agreed to meet them at a truck stop outside of town and give them a lift to wherever they needed to go. Theo decided to wait to tell his friend in person what the next step was, just in case.

Naya didn't say much as they walked toward the truck stop. Theo didn't mind. The anticipation felt more reassuring than any meaningless small talk. In fact, she didn't utter more than a few words until Benny drove up in his little beater sedan. Then she arched one elegant brow at Theo.

"You want me to get into that death trap?" she asked.

Theo was smiling before he could nod. "It's a far cry better than wandering around aimlessly. And rats have good hearing by the way."

No expression gave away her thoughts on the matter, but Theo could've sworn he saw a muscle twitch at the corner of Naya's eye as they climbed into the car. Naya took the back seat and Theo climbed into the front passenger seat with a fist bump from his friend.

"Since when have you swapped sides my man?" Benny had never mastered the fine art of subtlety.

"What sides?" Naya asked from the back seat with a bit of alarm in her voice.

"You know, he always played for the other team. I never thought I'd see him hooked up with a gal, especially one as pretty as you." He wagged his eyebrows at Naya via the rear view mirror.

Theo pinched the bridge of his nose.

"Oh." Naya hesitated for an awkward amount of time before adding, "He has a potential mate, and it's not me. I could see how you could make that conclusion, but it would be incorrect."

"Dang man, where'd you find the rules lawyer?" Benny chuckled as he turned off the highway.

"Cool it Benny. We have a situation and I need you to do me a solid. Please tell me you know how to find the local wolf pack?" Theo barely got his hands braced against the dash in time to prevent his face from bouncing off of it as Benny hit the brakes.

"What the hell man? What kind of trouble are you trying to bring my way?" Benny half turned in his seat to look at Theo with wild eyed panic worn openly on his face.

Theo had forgotten how flighty and easily excitable rats could be. The trait kept them alive, but could sometimes make it really hard to get things done. "Benny, calm down. This is serious."

"Excuse me, but I don't think we should linger in the middle of the road." Naya spoke calmly from the backseat.

Benny shot Naya a brief glare over his shoulder, but then continued driving down the road. After a few blocks of silence, during which Theo's heart made a valiant effort to beat out of his chest, Benny smacked his palm against the steering wheel.

"For Christ's sake Theo, what could possibly be so important that you want to willingly mess with wolves?" Benny closed both hands on the steering wheel, making his knuckles go white.

"Fynn. He's in trouble." Theo knew he wouldn't need more of an explanation than that.

Rubbing a hand over his forehead, Benny slouched in his seat. "Well shit."

"Come on, I know you've gotten the lay of the land by now. You have to tell me where they are. Fynn should've been home by now if the pack had simply turned him away. Something ain't right." Theo pushed down on the unease making his legs quiver, rubbing dampness onto his sweats with equally shaky hands.

Benny seemed to make a decision and took a sharp right without signaling. "Alright, here's the deal. A little while back there was some big to do between the Alpha of the pack, a witch, and the local Enforcer. The Alpha died and ever since there's been a constant fight for top dog. It's even caused a lot of the other shifters to vacate the area, cuz the Enforcer can't seem to pin the pack down. They move around, you see, and never squat at the same place twice. But I happen to know where they are now. Aren't I lucky."

"What are they doing to make people leave?" as he asked, Theo noted Naya leaning forward in her seat.

"All I know is it has to do with the supernatural black market, and the wolf who ended up on top. I've been trying to stay below their radar. Like sewers kind of below. But it's hard to ignore the smell." Benny shivered, as if he could still smell what he described.

The next few blocks, and a right turn, passed in a heavy silence. Eventually Benny pulled over and turned off the car. He kept his hands on the steering wheel and Theo watched the inner struggle play out in the set of Benny's jaw, the rise and fall of his shallow breaths, and the increasing furrow of his brow. Benny wasn't the bravest person in the world, but he was loyal, and it was obvious those two sides were at war with each other,

"Theo, my man, you need to be careful. These wolves aren't to be trusted. They're into some weird shit to chase the shifters away. I hope you find Fynn, and I hope the little dude is all right." He finally turned toward Theo. "Their building is the second one on this block. You can go up the alley, or around the front and to the right. I don't know your plan, but there are always at least two guards."

Theo nodded, glancing back at Naya, who lowered her eyes and stepped out of the car. He turned back to Benny and held out his hand. "Thanks man. I'll hit you up some time."

Benny quirked a small smile. "Yeah, totally. See ya around."

They shook hands and Theo climbed out. Tension bunched in his shoulders as he watched the sedan disappear down the road. Naya shifted her weight from foot to foot, clenching her hands at her sides.

"Is there protocol for a situation like this?" Theo asked.

Naya shook her head. "The local Enforcer already knows that we're here to see the wolf pack. And once we headed toward them, I put him on alert through my phone, so he knows where we are. He says he's over an hour away. But this is dangerous and we don't have time to wait for backup. I can feel the certainty of that fact."

The tension in his back began to burn in his muscles. Yeah, he could feel it too. "So I guess we just walk up and knock then. Maybe they'll negotiate with us."

The swan shifter simply stared at him, wide-eyed and practically vibrating as she fidgeted. Theo couldn't turn back. His mom expected him to bring back his brother, so that's what he planned to do. Since it was nearest, he chose to take the alley. Naya followed close, her heat melding with Theo's.

Two men stepped out from between the buildings. Both appeared to have coordinated their outfits, as they each wore loose-fit jeans and black T-shirts. One took a wide stance, crossing his arms and glaring. The other stayed relaxed, and he was the one to speak. "You lost?"

Theo tried to loosen up, taking his example from the wolf who spoke. "Nah, I'm looking for my brother. I was told he came to speak to your boss about getting some help."

The one with his arms crossed laughed. "He does resemble the little feather duster."

Anger sparked at the insult, but Theo tried not to react as the two shared a laugh.

"But who's this? She don't smell like you, more like a turkey. You a turkey little girl?" The first guy to speak pointed at Naya.

"She's my girlfriend, and loves the shit out of my lil bro." Adopting the assumption Benny had made was the first thing that popped into his head.

"I guess if they want to talk to the boss, we should oblige them. Kaido, stay here. I'll be back."

Kaido, the one who'd called Fynn a feather duster, nodded and stepped back so the other wolf could lead them to the door. His glare followed them until Theo broke eye contact to keep track of the man in front of him. He'd have to hold out hope of making the smug thug eat his words. When they entered the building all thoughts of insults fled, replaced by the stench of blood, both old and new. Theo tried not to react, but the smell made him want to retch. Benny hadn't exaggerated one bit. They made their way through a maze of hallways until their escort made a sharp turn and a large room opened up. A small port-hole showed the mountains in the distance, but there were no other windows. That was the only detail Theo gleaned before his gaze fell on Fynn, arms spread and caught in between human and eagle. His flight feathers had been plucked and were arranged in a case on a metal table in front of the wooden panel he'd been strung up on.

"Fynn!" Theo lunged for his brother and took a blow to the side of his head. He tumbled to the ground as his momentum carried him further into the room. Naya was beside him before he could tell up from down.

"Nice, you brought me an adult eagle to replace the juvenile there." A man stepped into Theo's skewed line of sight. He was tall and decked out much like his underlings. "And to top the cake, he brought an Enforcer with him to watch while we drain all of the blood they have to offer. She can be a good little messenger and finally get that owl out of our fur. In exchange, maybe we don't rough her up… too much."

Naya's hands bunched in Theo's shirt. If he could smell her fear, and knew the wolves could too.

Chapter Sixteen

JAMES SAT in Eluna's private jet as it left the small airport outside Billings. He'd never liked planes, even when they'd been necessary as an Enforcer. Leaving the ground not under his own power was strange and a little disorienting. The world fell away and he was suspended in mid air, not able to feel the wind on his face or ride the currents in the sky. He didn't know what was worse, leaving his cabin in the mountains, or flying in a machine. If it hadn't been for Theo, he wouldn't have done either. Even looking out the window of the plane felt strange and alien.

Eluna pulled her phone away from her ear and frowned. "They already reached New Mexico. According to the local Enforcer, Naya contacted him almost an hour ago to advise him they were going after the local werewolf pack."

James frowned. "The local werewolf pack? Why on earth would they go after a werewolf pack? Naya's truth sensing powers won't help her with werewolves. And Theo doesn't have any combat training that I know of." As he said the words, he realized he didn't really know much about Theo, aside from the unmistakably strong attraction between the two of them, a connection strong enough it could only be called a developing mate bond.

"Sounds like Theo's little brother went to them about something, that's still unclear. Maybe he's looking for protection from the Enforcers and thinks a pack can offer him that." Eluna shook her head. "I've tried calling Naya's phone, but there's no answer. She may be in the middle of something."

"Or they might be in trouble," James finished for her. He kept flashing back to the vision he'd had, his first in years. Theo was going to be in bad shape or worse when they found them. He wished there was something he could do to make the jet fly faster. "How long is it going to take us to get there?"

"Let me check with the pilot, but I seem to recall around two hours. We're lucky there aren't any storms tonight, so we can make good time." Eluna stood and walked up to the cockpit, leaving James to his own thoughts.

He couldn't believe his life had turned so far upside down in just a few days. But he'd gotten an answer to the biggest question of his life, only to have more questions pop up. He'd known Orville was a power-hungry bureaucrat, but he'd never dreamed he'd have ordered James' family destroyed all for the desire of removing James as a rival. If they all survived rescuing Theo and his brother from the wolves, he wanted to get to the bottom of Orville's deceit. Maybe if all his questions were answered he could finally let his family know he was still alive, and let them meet Theo. He *had* to be fast enough to reach Theo, he just had to.

Eluna came back from the cockpit. "Will says we'll be in Albuquerque in an hour and a half. The problem is that once we land, we're still going to have to find them. I called Shannon back, you remember the European Eagle Owl who was in Enforcer training about the same time you were? He says he's got a trace lock on Naya's phone. She asked him to watch out for her. But it's going to take him an hour or so to get free to head down there. Something about a stand off with a drunk man in a bar."

James remembered the cheerful redheaded man. "Stand off with a drunk? What is he a sheriff or something?"

"Exactly. As an Enforcer, he doesn't get a ton of work in New Mexico, so he doubles as a small-town sheriff. The only reason we had two operatives there was due to the area that needed to be covered. Shannon said as soon as they get everything sorted out up in the mountains, he and his partners will be on their way. We're to call him when we land, or he'll call us when they reach town." Eluna settled back in the seat across from James. "Maybe we can sort out a few things as we fly. It'll help take our minds off the situation at hand."

James didn't honestly want to take his mind off the coming conflict. He wanted to focus on it. He wanted to dig into his precognitive gift and figure out exactly what would happen, but he knew if he overthought things he'd make a mistake that, when dealing with a pack of werewolves, could be disastrous. She also wasn't giving him much of a choice. "Where would you like me to start?"

Eluna took out a laptop and opened it up. "How about when Orville gave you the assignment?" She poised her hands over the keyboard.

With a sigh, he began laying out everything as he remembered it. It was a difficult tale to get out, since it had been the hardest thing he'd ever done. He'd been foolish to believe simply faking his death would be enough and worried about what else Orville had been up to when he hadn't been there to keep an eye on him. James realized he might've been able to save a few lives if he'd stayed and fought, and he wouldn't have had to put his family through the pain of his loss.

James felt pretty confident that Orville wouldn't have stopped until he got what he wanted. There really was no way of knowing what damage he would've caused if James had made a stand. As he continued his tale, the pain in his heart grew knowing there had to be others who'd suffered simply because they were more notable than a jealous rival.

They began their descent into Albuquerque and James was fairly satisfied he had Eluna on his side. But he also knew he would have to replay everything to the full Enforcer council. At one point, Eluna had paused to get them both water, during which time she'd made another phone call and requested the council convene as soon as possible.

When they touched down, Eluna called Shannon and was informed he was still a good forty five minutes out. The standoff ended badly, and the state patrol had been called in and slowed things down. He gave Eluna the current coordinates of Naya's phone and she pulled it up as soon as she ended the call.

There was a large black SUV waiting for them at the bottom of the ramp as they got off the plane.

"Wouldn't it be faster to fly?" James said, anxious to be off.

Eluna shook her head. "It's night. Neither one of us has the best night vision, and this is the wrong time of year for sandhill cranes to be in New Mexico. We ride. We only shift if we have to, is that understood?"

As much as James wanted to argue, she had a point. He knew his limitations, but he couldn't shake the cold fist of terror that clenched his heart. Theo was in deep trouble and he had to get there fast.

Eluna gave the driver the address as they climbed into the SUV.

"We'll be there in ten minutes, ma'am," the driver said as she pulled away from the curb.

"Find a parking lot within a block or two," Eluna instructed. "We've got back up coming."

"Of course."

James wondered where the driver had come from. He couldn't catch a good look at her to try to determine her species, but he was surprised by the opulence Eluna traveled in. Back in the day, the Elite Enforcers weren't so elegant. Maybe it had to do with her being a crane. He knew some shifters tended to need more in the way of flashy things than others.

James stayed quiet as they drove through the evening streets of Albuquerque. Traffic was less than James expected, but they weren't going into one of the better parts of town by the looks of it. The farther they drove, the more James wanted to rush to Theo's side. He started to feel fear and pain that couldn't be his own. It reminded him of the tales of mates and their close bonds. Some bonded mates could feel everything the other one did. He and Theo weren't close; they hadn't had time to become incredibly close, but he could still feel pain. Every so often, it felt like someone was ripping feathers out. The pain started at the tips of his fingers and flowed along his hands and arms. It shot through him, and urged James to find whoever was torturing Theo and destroy them. He had to utilize all of his meditation techniques in order to keep from having an outward reaction every time a spike hit.

"Will this do, ma'am?" the driver asked as they pulled into a grocery store that had a half-full parking lot.

"Perfect," Eluna said as the driver turned off the SUV. She pulled out her phone. "We've arrived. We're at a small local grocery store about a block east of the address. We'll see-"

James didn't wait for her to finish what she was saying to Shannon. He opened his door and started walking west. It was the direction his instincts were telling him to go anyway.

"James, wait!" Eluna shouted after him.

"No. There's no time." He yelled back before picking up his pace until he was running.

The pull from Theo turned him down an alley. Two men stepped out in front of him. His precognitive powers kicked in. He could see they were both werewolves from the way they moved in perfect coordination with each other, but it didn't help them.

"Hey!" one hollered at him. "What do you--"

James slammed his fist into the man's jaw as he tried pulling a glock from his jacket. The other man shot at him, but James swung the first wolf around to take the bullet instead. The years of rust from disuse fell away, and he could see everything seconds before it happened.

The shots brought three more wolves running out a door just down the alley. James knew he had to be faster than they were. He slid behind the door mere seconds before they opened it. Using the door as a shield, James took the opportunity to take out one of the wolves and slammed the door shut hard, catching the man between the door and the frame with a resounding crack that shattered most of his ribs and broke his back. Using the door handle as a brace, James swung a high kick into the head of the wolf who'd entered the alley ahead of the one he'd taken out with the door. The man's head snapped back and he fell down even as James leapt over him, spun in mid-air as he half shifted, and impacted between the first wolf's shoulder blades to knock him to the ground.

James' power showed him two more men running down the hall beyond the door toward the alley. He shifted back to human form and paused as several possible futures played out in his mind. In all of them he took at least one bullet. His best option presented itself and he moved to be in the right position to only take a shot to the shoulder, and not one to the head or heart.

The door flew open, dropping the gravely injured man to the ground. James leapt to the left, and as his gift showed him, the wolves were already firing. A bullet clipped his left shoulder. It knocked him back a couple of feet, but the impact wasn't enough to stop him, even as silver burned into his flesh. He used the inertia from the gunshot to spin into the wall opposite the door, and kicked off the concrete. He flipped over the two men still trying to shoot him. As soon as his feet hit the ground, he used one jump to kick first the left shooter in the temple and then the right. They crumpled close to the other fallen wolves as James ducked into the dim hallway.

The hall was quiet as he entered. His power still thrummed in the back of his mind, ready to show him what would come even as his shoulder burned with the silver coursing through his system. If he'd been anything but a golden eagle with healing blood, he'd have dropped to the floor in complete agony. He still needed to get the bullet out. But before he could do that, he had to find Theo.

His powers warned him to run, right before a door opened and a large wolf barreled down the hall. James didn't turn around since the brute ran in the wrong direction. He had three minutes before the wolf realized his error, that would be more than enough time for him to find the alpha and take him out.

The hall was a winding labyrinth of shifting directions, but James followed his powers. A door opened and he was ready to kill the wolf who came sniffing out more cautiously than the ones in the alley had been. His cautious attitude was his undoing as James slammed him into the wall with a sick thud. Then, with the smell of shifter blood nearly overwhelming him, James stood at the last door. Theo and Naya were just beyond that barrier. There were four more wolves in there with them and several other eagles who were close to or already dead. The dead threw off his precognitive power, presenting spots of darkness and obstacles he couldn't see around. One of the forms kept flickering from alive to dead, depending on how James went into the room. Selecting the most positive outcome, James flung the door open and rushed in. Bullets zipped in his direction. His power showed him one of the wolves moving toward Theo. He aimed for that one first. It didn't matter who the wolf was, he would hurt Theo if James didn't get there first. Half shifting, James launched himself across the room. His clothes impeded his movement, but his body was lighter for half of the jump, so he went further. He slammed into the man as he shifted back to man, then ducked as another one shot at him. Grabbing the man by the shoulders, James spun and used him as a shield so bullets tore into him. When his gift told him the time was right, James threw the shredded wolf at the attacker. They collided and hit the floor. James was already in motion again, driven by his gift to move to the left and take out the man who'd been slowly, at least to his gift, pulling a 9mm from his belt. He was the last real threat in the room. James hit his gun hand, breaking his wrist, then slammed the Alpha into the wall by the throat.

"Your pack is neutralized. You're finished." James spoke for the first time since his power took him over. But even as the words left his mouth, an image appeared in his mind of the council putting him in chains and Theo crying hysterically. He opened his hands and let the stunned Alpha fall to the floor.

Slowly, the future receded and James rushed to Theo's side.

Without his power controlling him, the pain in James' shoulder was immense. He did his best to ignore the burn as he reached Theo who lay on an examining table with tubes poked into his arms where his flight feathers should be. Close by was a teenage boy who looked like a younger version of Theo. Fynn. He had a similar rigging trailing from his arms as well. The tubes collected blood and carried it to jars for collection. The other eagle shifters were hooked up the same way, each stuck in their half forms and their feathers laid out on the tables around them.

"Theo." James touched Theo's forehead. "Please Theo, tell me you're going to be alright."

"They're going to need blood," Naya said, approaching from the chair she'd been tied to. She rubbed her wrists, as if trying to put her joints back into normal alignment after popping them to allow her to slip her hands free of her bonds. Her face was beaten black and blue. Her shirt hung in tatters.

"I've been shot with silver," James said. "Mine won't be any good to anyone until I can get the bullet out and have time to cleanse my system."

"Let us handle the clean up." Eluna entered the room, looking like she was about to be ill. "You could've waited for help, James. There was only one wolf, who looked oddly confused, left to stand in our way."

"There was no time," James said as he pulled the tubes for Theo's arms. "I knew if we waited too long, there'd be too much damage done. As it is, it's going to take Theo a while to wake up, the others even longer. They're all drained. That one." He pointed to the young woman on the far table. "She's going to need help to wake up. Even once she's unplugged from all of this, it'll be at least a day before she wakes. I left the Alpha alive." He waved in the direction of the wolf still crumpled against the wall. "The rest couldn't be spared without risk to the lives involved."

He touched Theo's face and desperately wanted him to wake up and smile. The strange merging of raptor and human features didn't allow for any hope of a smile. They'd won the fight, but he knew there was still a lot to get done.

"I've heard legends about how you use your precognitive gift to enhance your fighting skills, but never expected to see it in action," Naya said. "It's something I'll never forget."

"And I hope to never have to use it again," James said. He wanted to bundle Theo up and disappear again, but he knew that wasn't an option. The Enforcers were back in his life and things were going to be complicated. He just hoped they'd be able to work out something that would leave everyone happy.

Chapter Seventeen

THEO STRUGGLED against the wall keeping him from waking up. He was cognitive enough to wonder if the wolves used some kind of sedative crafted specifically for shifters. But then arms slid underneath him and lifted him off the hard surface, shattering the wall and allowing him to crack his eyes open. James smiled down at him.

"And here I thought I'd woken up. I must still be dreaming, because you're in Montana. But I like this dream." Theo would never give up in such dire circumstance, especially with Fynn in danger, and yet he wanted to simply lie in James' arms till the end claimed him.

"Shhh, don't talk like that. I'm here, I've got you. Both you and Fynn are going to be okay." James pulled Theo closer to his chest.

The mention of Fynn got Theo's attention. There were people moving around beyond his line of sight, and the smell of blood caked the back of his throat. When he moved his nose to keep from sneezing, Theo felt the difference in his facial features and his breath caught. Before he could cry out in panic though, Naya appeared to his left and laid a hand on his arm.

"Theo, how bad are you hurt?" she asked.

"Fynn?" Theo responded.

"He's not coherent, Naya, don't excite him until we can get everyone out of here." James moved to walk around Naya, but she stepped in the way.

The two glared at each other over Theo's upturned face. A sudden pang of anxiety left Theo nauseous. "Please guys, don't fight."

His pathetic words evoked an instant reaction. The tension drained out of James' shoulders and Naya smiled down at him.

"Don't worry about your brother. Those wolves have been testing out a more potent tranquilizer for shifters, but I heard the lie in the Alpha's words when he said it lasted a long time. Fynn should come to very soon, if he hasn't already." She touched his face. "Your mother will be very happy to see you both."

Theo couldn't care less about going anywhere. His head rested against James' chest and the heartbeat filling his ears made everything else secondary. He offered Naya a smile and she moved away. James began walking again as soon as she got out of his way, and he carried Theo through the dank building. Fresh air brushed his face the moment they stepped into the alley, drawing a sigh from deep in Theo's chest. Relief at being away from the stench of torture made him feel a little giddy.

"Theo!"

In a burst of motion faster than Theo could follow, Fynn pushed through a pair of grim looking shifters and James maneuvered Theo upright onto his feet to catch his brother without toppling them all to the ground. The weight of Fynn's gangly body in Theo's arms, added to the reassuring grip of James holding him steady, chased away whatever cobwebs still lingered. Only then did Theo acknowledge the fear he'd been carrying since the day he'd left to lead the Enforcers away. The same kind of fear he'd felt when he had to turn away and leave James in Montana.

They held each other for a long while, and Theo happily noted where James' hand stayed—firmly on Theo's lower back, the entire time. He held Fynn away from him by the shoulders and made no effort to wipe away the tears streaming down his face.

With a smile on his face, he ruffled Fynn's already messy hair. "You little idiot, you scarred the life out of me! What were you thinking?"

"I had to do something. Those people were after you and it was all my fault. Don't be mad." His dark brows knitted together in what Theo knew to be Fynn's worried face.

"Never. Never mad. But hey, I have someone I'd like you to meet. Fynn, this is James." Theo motioned to where James stood.

Fynn glanced at the shorter man and his eyes went wide. "Hey, aren't you the one everyone's talking about? You know, the scary Enforcer Elite guy or something like that?"

James' face went blank and he swallowed hard.

Theo nodded. "Yes, that would be him."

"Oh man! Everyone is talking about how you fought all these wolves by yourself! And I heard you shifted back and forth between eagle and man, throwing kicks and dodging shots before they were even fired! That's so cool, you have to teach me how to do that!"

Fynn mimed fighting an invisible foe as if he could mimic the motions James had done.

Did James fight the entire werewolf pack to save him and his brother?

The pulse in Theo's neck spiked and he waited for some kind of reaction from James. Slowly, as Fynn continued his antics, the deer-in-the-headlights expression faded from James' face and was replaced with a warm smile.

Before anyone else could speak, an elderly woman walked up, flanked by more of the grim looking shifters. Theo guessed she was a big-to-do with the Enforcers and tried to stand up straight, but instead ended up leaning against James as his knees wobbled. The contact was a welcome comfort.

"Hello, Theo and Fynn Montoya. I'm Eluna, one of the council members governing the Enforcers. After having a brief word with my colleagues, as well as Naya, I would like to take you both home to have a talk with your mother about the current situation. They have given us two days to sort things out, and then I must take James to his full trial in front of the leaders of the International Shifter Committee." She motioned toward the open door of a large, black SUV.

Theo looked at James sharply. In the haze of things he'd totally forgotten the fact that James was in trouble. "I thought you would've had that all cleared up. They let you leave the tribunal?"

"Extenuating circumstances came to light." James averted his eyes, but kept his hand firmly on Theo's back.

"Yes, we now have a council member to investigate. But it was paramount for James to get to you in time, Theo. You won't find many shifters who are willing to stand in the way of protecting a mate." Eluna smiled as if she hadn't just confirmed the fact Theo had tried to convince himself of otherwise the entire flight to Santa Fe. But there was no way the council woman could know that.

"Wait, they're mates? Nobody told me!" Fynn crossed his arms, his bottom lip protruding in such a way to make him appear the petulant child.

Theo's face grew hot and a lump formed in his throat. He wanted to crack a joke or something to break the tension, but nothing witty came to mind.

"Well, we—I…" James struggled to form the words.

"We never finished bonding. So we're not truly mated." Theo meant to say yet, but the word refused to form. He hadn't even meant to say the words out loud, but the part of him still feeling hurt and rejected came shining through, before James could say it instead.

James' hand fell away from Theo's back and he instantly felt cold. He stepped towards Fynn and wrapped an arm over his brother's shoulders. "Come on, let's go home. Mom's going to have a fit when she sees our clothes."

A second vehicle arrived to take the injured eagles to the closest healer, so the ride back to Santa Fe was less cramped than it could've been. As it was, Naya rode up front with the driver and Eluna, and Fynn sat between James and Theo in the back seat. Time seemed to crawl as they drove, and Theo stayed silent in spite of the pull in every molecule of his body reaching for James. Fynn bounced his knee in place, almost as if he could feel the energy and it made him jumpy. When they finally pulled up outside of Theo's home, he was so exhausted that he missed his mom standing in the drive. She pulled open the back door and yanked Theo out, followed shortly by Fynn.

"Aye, my boys!" She crushed them in a hug that, with her short stature, should've been physically impossible. But each of her arms encircled both the necks of Theo and Fynn, effectively pinning them to her shoulders.

Theo refused to acknowledge the pain, and shook his head at his brother when Fynn opened his mouth to let out some kind of cry. Mariposa needed to feel her sons' safe in her arms, and he'd lie across coals to give her any reassurance she needed.

The reunion didn't last as long as it should've, because Eluna cleared her throat. "Excuse me, Mrs. Montoya?"

Mariposa stood, somehow managing to sweep her boys behind her as she squared off with the council woman. "It's Ms. Montoya."

"Ms. My apologies. I'm--"

"I know who you are, and you can keep your apologies," his mom said.

If Theo didn't know any better, he'd think Mariposa was the shifter parent, instead of their deadbeat dad. Theo swore he could see fire flicker in his mother's eyes.

"Look, I know this isn't the best of circumstances, but—" Eluna began.

Mariposa held her hand up. "Please spare me the friendly speech. You're here to threaten my sons, and I find that detestable. You're going to ask to sit in my house, drink my coffee, and try to tell me that you're going to punish first my youngest for protecting himself, and then my oldest for trying to protect his younger brother. I won't have it."

"Mom…" Theo worried that his mother didn't have all the facts, but she held a hand up to him as well.

Naya stepped forward. "Excuse me ma'am. I'm the one who was originally sent to assess this case. I have new information to present."

A glare formed on Mariposa's face, until she got a good look at Naya. "Oh my goodness! Did those wolves do that to you?" She made a disgusted sound deep in her throat. "May they all get fleas! Come inside, I'll get you some ice for your face."

As Mariposa turned away, Naya cleared her throat. "Um, may we *all* come in?"

Theo's mom didn't even stop, she simply waved them forward. "Yes, of course! For you dear, only for you. I'll put on some coffee."

No one spoke while Mariposa fussed over Naya. In fact, there was a pointed silence until everyone was sitting in their small living room, with a coffee or some kind of drink, and Theo's mom sat herself in her recliner.

"Alright my dear, tell me about this new information." She looked at Naya as she sipped her almost white coffee.

Naya smiled and pulled the ice pack from her cheek. "Well, while the wolves were boasting about how clever they were, one of the lower wolves congratulated the Alpha on setting Fynn up in the first place. The Alpha agreed and said he never expected to be able to bag two eagles at the expense of one overly zealous human trying to prove he could run with the pack. I'm paraphrasing of course, because I prefer not to curse the way those wolves did."

The room grew quiet again. So many thoughts rushed through Theo's mind, and he still felt like he was fighting through a haze to comprehend it all. They'd been set up from the start. But if they hadn't been, James would never have walked into his life. Should he be grateful to the wolves for trying to kill them?

Each person in the room eventually looked at Mariposa. Even Eluna seemed to be waiting for a response before speaking. His mom took one last sip and set down her cup.

"Well, thank you my dear. That settles it. My sons will be fully pardoned and no action will be taken against them." She smoothed out the wrinkles in her pants, as if she were brushing away the subject like so much unwanted dirt.

Eluna stood then, her hands facing palms out. "As much as I'm leaning towards agreeing with you, what with Naya being a truth seeker and all, I can't just sweep this under the proverbial rug. The proper channels have to be followed, or else someone could take this matter up in the future."

Mariposa stood as well. How she managed to be shorter and still talk down to a person of authority, Theo would never quite understand. "So you will follow the proper channels and make sure my sons are never punished for their actions, but they'll be staying here. Fynn has missed out on too much as it is, and Theo's work has been missing him. They should be allowed to return to their lives."

"I would love to let them do that," Eluna looked over at Theo. "But I have to return with James for his own part in all of this, and it would be helpful to have at least Theo there to answer questions for the council."

Theo didn't need any more of a hint. He stood and added his larger frame to the crowded feel of people standing in a small space. "Mom, James risked his life to save me and Fynn, as well as other eagle shifters the wolf pack took. And all this trouble because our blood had the potential to make the pack money on the black market." He'd put two and two together, even though no one had seemed to want to say it out loud. "I want to go with him."

Theo's words hung heavy in the air, even after he stopped speaking. The fight that could've been brewing with his mom dissipated, just like it had when she saw Naya. Theo let out the breath he'd been holding and swayed. His mom was there with a gentle arm around his waist.

"Okay, that's enough for today. You need to lie down, and I'm sure your brother needs rest too. They'll all still be here when you wake up." She steered him back towards his room.

Before they walked down the hall, Theo glanced over his shoulder. His heart sank at the downcast expression James wore, and pain lanced through his chest at the shattered hope that James would've followed them to make sure he was all right.

Chapter Eighteen

JAMES BARELY kept himself from running after Theo. He knew he couldn't look. Just the sight of Theo being led off to bed by his mother would be James' undoing. The words Theo spoke, about them not being mated, still echoed in his head and kept him stubbornly glued to the spot.

Eluna turned, placing her hands on her hips, and a mothering scowl worn openly on her face. "Well now. I know it's not my place to say, and after the success of the previous conversation I risk looking more like an idiot, but you shouldn't let hurt feelings keep you from sealing your bond."

"I'll take it from here." Mariposa strode back into the room, commanding the same respect as a four star general. "James, I'm going to put Fynn to bed as well, and then I'd like you to walk with me." She had Fynn up and moving even as she finished talking.

Eluna shrugged at James, as if to say he was on his own. Naya simply looked away. James stood and stepped out the front door. The cramped space did nothing to calm his nerves, and he expected that Mariposa would know where to find him. He let the cool air run over him and leaned against the side of the trailer.

Night had fallen and the stars filled the sky. As seen in the city as opposed to in his forest, they weren't as bright and brilliant, but they were still there. He'd give anything to be holding Theo, lying beneath either sky. The door creaked open and Mariposa's scent surrounded James.

"I'm not one for metaphors or passing along wisdom. And I've never seen my son stand up for anyone besides his family. He's had to be the man, ever since he was small. His daddy was in and out of his life, right up until Fynn was born, then he disappeared. Theo felt like he had to take care of us after that. Helping me carry groceries and cook meals, and beating up the bullies who picked on his brother in school. He even made sure he got a job right out of high school, so he could help me pay the bills. My poor miho, he should've been going off to college and figuring out what he wanted to do with his life." She stopped and took a deep breath.

James wouldn't have broken that silence for all the money in the world. What she told him had been a huge mystery since Theo crashed into his forest. He wanted nothing more than to hear whatever else she would give him about the man he loved.

"Do you love him?" she asked.

He snapped his head around to look her in the eyes. With how close their thoughts were, he had to wonder if she was telepathic. Her eyebrow arched and he realized he'd forgotten to answer her.

"Yes." The word seemed too simplistic to cover his emotions, but it was all his throat would let him get out at that moment.

She smiled. "Then what's stopping you?"

With it laid so plainly in front of him, James honestly didn't have an answer for the question. He wanted to be with Theo. He knew in the core of his soul they were connected. And he'd never been so alive as their first night together. Though his cheeks flushed to think about such things in front of Theo's mom. He swallowed the lump forming in his throat.

Mariposa stepped forward and cupped James' face in a warm grasp. "It's okay to be afraid. Aye dios mio, I'd be worried if you weren't afraid. But don't make him wait for you for the rest of his life, like my Quinn did to me. Find a way to be happy."

James grinned. "I'll do my best, ma'am."

"Good." Mariposa let go of him and stepped back. "And if you don't, I'm going to find you, pluck you and leave you for the buzzards."

"Got it." James gulped and had no doubt that if he ever intentionally hurt Theo she'd do just that.

"Mom, I'm an adult and you really don't have to defend me like this." Theo appeared out of the house's shadows.

"You're my boy, of course I do." Mariposa walked up to him and kissed his cheek. "Now you two go talk for a while, or whatever. It's been a long day and I think I'm going to go draw it out a little while longer for those Enforcer ladies before I let them get any sleep. And I expect *you* to make sure he doesn't overexert himself, since he should be resting." She grinned at James and strolled back toward the house.

James didn't pity either Naya or Eluna when Mariposa got back in there, although caring for Naya had occupied her for a while, she obviously had more to say to them. He waited in silence until she closed the door and disappeared. "She's a strong woman. I don't want to end up on her bad side."

"You've got no idea," Theo said, stepping close enough to wrap his arm around James' waist. "Mother tigers have nothing on my mom. When she says she'll pluck you, be thankful she didn't threaten to roast you afterwards. I heard her tell my dad that more than once."

James shuddered. "Yeah. Keep the very dangerous woman happy."

Theo laughed. "If you keep me happy, you'll be keeping her happy, too."

"Then we should be in the clear." James leaned his head against Theo's shoulder. "I'm going to do everything I can to keep you happy. We might not know each other very well, but I feel the bond between us and through it, I feel you. And you feel great."

"So do you." Theo turned James in his arms so they could kiss. It was a long sensual kiss that sent waves of heat up and down James as they stood there in the darkness.

"What now?" James asked as their lips parted. He wanted to leave with Theo and not have to worry about the Enforcers and their BS. He just wanted to focus on Theo and their life together.

"We can't just fly away can we? I tried that already and although I found you, it didn't exactly end well for others."

James ran his hands through Theo's hair and grinned up at him. "Not really. I think we need to work everything out first, and then worry about the rest of our lives.”

“Sounds good.” Theo said. “So do you think anyone would notice if we disappeared for a little while, as long as we’re back before breakfast?”

James liked the idea that popped into his mind, if he was going to the same place Theo was. “And how early is breakfast?”

Theo sighed and shook his head. “A lot earlier than I’d like to admit. But if we get into the air, maybe we can slip away quickly.”

“Good.”

The night was still clear as James let go of Theo’s hand. There was a beautiful three-quarter moon just rising over the horizon as James disrobed, visualizing his eagle form, and dropped his human guise. The light would be enough for him to find his way, even if his eagle’s night vision was a little worse than his human sight. He cleared the trees when he realized Theo was beside him. Theo beat his wings, angling higher into the night sky.

James followed Theo up. Their previous flight had been utilitarian compared to how he felt as they went to lofty heights above Santa Fe. Theo stopped going up and started circling. Every so often the lights from the city flickered off the white patches in his wings. James made it to Theo’s elevation and joined him in the last lingering thermal of the day. The warm air current carried them a little higher before giving out. James had never flown with another shifter for the sole reason of enjoying the air and each other.

With a high pitched shriek, Theo flew toward James. He made a close pass, holding out his talons like a wild eagle would for a food exchange. James stared, wondering what Theo was trying to get at. On the third time, when Theo's talons brushed James', he got the idea.

Theo circled up above him again, and then swooped in. James rolled at just the right moment and grabbed hold of Theo's talons in his own. The movement jarred them both, and for a split second James thought about letting go, but he'd watched wild eagles do what they were trying, and it felt right. The part of his brain that sought to close their mate bond sang as they started to fall from the sky. James angled his wings like he'd see other birds do. As Theo copied his move, it pulled them out of their tumble. They shared the danger of crashing into the ground, but also the thrill of holding on while they spun like a giant dark pinwheel. The very forces of their spin fought to yank them apart and send them rolling through the sky. They held on tightly to each other, like they would need to do in life if they were going to make it through together.

As the ground came closer and closer, their trust in each other grew. James was aware of how powerful Theo was. Even if Theo didn't believe he was strong. There was a light in Theo that needed to be fanned so it would grow. Together they could accomplish great things, they just had to trust one another to be there whenever they were needed. They had to rely on the fact they were meant to be one spirit.

They were nearly at tree level when Theo's hold on James' talons lessened. Then James let go, and his heart cried out about no longer touching Theo. He spread his wings and soared back into the sky. Theo followed him. They circled back into the sky. Theo swooped close to James. They locked talons again. When they reached the tree level again they let go and flew down to the ground.

James shifted and turned to find Theo rushing toward him. James caught him in his arms and hugged him tight.

"That was incredible," Theo said. "I've never felt anything like this before."

"Me either." James kissed him. Their lips burned as they lingered. He wanted to throw Theo down in the small woodlot where they landed and ravage him. The lust bellowed up inside him.

"Now," Theo muttered in James' ear.

James took the hint and hoped Theo knew the area enough that they wouldn't be disturbed. He needed to feel their bodies merging.

They were both nearly frantic, almost like the mate bond was riding them in their urge to complete it. James wanted desperately to take things slow and enjoy every inch of Theo, but the emptiness in his soul wasn't having any of it. He needed to be filled and made whole.

He nearly screamed as Theo pushed inside him. It felt so good. As Theo entered him, he kissed him long and hard. James rode Theo for all he was worth. He'd never had anyone who made him feel the way he did on the woodlot floor. If perfection existed, James knew in his heart it was in the way they felt together, skin to skin. He wanted it to go on forever, with Theo deep inside him and kissing him like a lovesick fool, but he knew that wasn't possible. The heat that engulfed them was nearly more than he could endure. The only thing that let him accept release was the knowledge he would be spending the rest of his life with Theo. He wasn't going to let anyone tear them apart.

The mate bond between them blazed like in miniature sun. Theo rammed himself into James deep and hard. Then he screamed, the long fierce cry of a joyous eagle from the throat of a man, as he came with explosive force. James came at the exact same time, as if compelled by the forming ties that were allowing him to feel Theo's pleasure. The power of their bonding wrapped itself around the two of them. In that moment, James wasn't sure where he ended and Theo began. They felt like a single entity.

Theo hugged James tightly as tears streaked down his cheeks and fell to mingle with James' cum on their chests.

James' heart clenched tight as they clung to each other. He never wanted to let Theo go. Even as Theo's cock inside him grew limp and James' cum cooled between them, he wanted to continue holding onto Theo.

Theo ran his hands through James' hair leaving tingles as he went. "That was incredible. I'm yours forever now, aren't I?"

James kissed his cheek, tasting the tears there. "Yes, just like I'm yours for the rest of our lives. I've never wanted anyone the way I want you."

"I feel the same way. But there's still so much we don't know about what's going to happen. The possibilities are endless."

"I know, but we're going to face it all together. I'm not going to let them do anything to tear us apart. I promise." James had dealt with the Enforcers many times before, but he'd never dealt with the Enforcer Council. He'd make them see that whatever they wanted of him, he was going to stay with Theo. He would fight for that the way he'd never fought for anything before.

Chapter Nineteen

THEO PACED the hall. The building was too clean, too neat, and he hated it. The Enforcers's headquarters was in a tall building in the middle of downtown Kansas City, Missouri. It seemed like a really stupid place to set up shop, at least until James had explained that the place was fairly close to the center of the United States. They both would've preferred Denver, but according to Eluna, Denver's weather could be more of a hindrance, particularly since a good number of the Enforcers had to fly in from other continents and winter weather could make travel difficult.

From the window at the end of the unremarkable hallway, the river was visible. Theo stopped there frequently as he paced the length of the building, waiting for the Enforcer Council to finish up with James' hearing. He'd given a short testimony about James' life in Montana, but hadn't been allowed to stay in the room. Even as James' mate, he wasn't privy to the secrets the Enforcers were throwing around.

When the door finally opened, Theo was at the far end of the hall, watching a pair of oneform falcons chase pigeons roosting on one of the bridges. He jerked around at the sound and raced down, not caring who saw him or what they thought.

Naya slumped with exhaustion as she entered the hallway. She looked like she'd just endured days of trauma and lived to tell about it.

"What's going on?" Theo asked, trying to glance around her, but the heavy wooden door was already closing.

She leaned against the wall and sighed. "James will be out in a moment and explain everything to you. We're going to need to go back to Santa Fe tonight."

Her statement didn't make any sense. "Santa Fe? Why Santa Fe? You're not taking me home, I belong with James."

Naya shook her head. "Yes you do. But that's not why we're going." She pushed off the wall. "I need to get a drink before we depart. I'll see you on the roof." And she walked off, leaving Theo to fume and wonder exactly what was going on.

The door opened again, and James walked out.

Theo turned and wrapped his arms around him, hugging him tight. "What happened? Naya looks horrible."

James gave him a quick kiss. "It was hard on her. She was the only Truth Seeker we could get here on such short notice. She had to make sure everyone was telling the truth, and some truths were harder to get than others." There was a dark quiet to James' voice Theo had never heard before.

"What do you mean?" Theo asked as the door opened again.

A short, squat man in an expensive suit came out. There was a strange leather collar around his neck that clashed with his clothes. It looked ancient, almost too brittle to be handled, let alone worn. He glared at James. "Was it worth it, Chan? Having everything laid out for you? How does it feel to know that your running was for nothing?"

In Theo's arms, James tensed. "Now it's worth it, Orville. You might've had my family killed even after I tried to save them, but you're forever grounded. You'll never fly again. You're going to be human until you die, and that's torture enough for any shifter."

"But you're an Enforcer again." Orville spat. "All your efforts were for naught."

James shook his head. "Not an *Enforcer*, a special agent. There's a difference." He pointed the two guards with Orville toward the elevator and then turned away.

"Wait, what just happened?" Theo asked.

"Let's walk. I need some air." James took Theo's hand and shuffled down the hall to the stairs leading one flight up to the roof. "Even after I disappeared to keep my family safe, Orville still had them killed. I failed them, but I won't fail you."

Theo stopped and looked back down the hall where the elevator dinged and Orville and his escort entered the lift that would take them somewhere else. "But he's bound now?"

James held the door to the stairs opened for Theo. "Yes. He's grounded. I'll never get my family back and it's taken all of my Buddhist training not to tear Orville's head off and leave him flopping on the floor like a dying fish. The things some people will do for political power. Orville was in charge of the Enforcers, and killed my family to ensure I could never challenge him for the position. What backwards thinking."

Their footsteps rang out hollowly as they went up the metal steps.

"You're a stronger man than I am," Theo said. "I'd have killed him regardless of the ramifications."

"When I was younger, before I spent all that time in the forest thinking my family was still alive and I might one day get to see them again, I might've killed him too. But if you spend enough time alone, you realize how special all life is, even the rotten pieces."

Theo opened the door for James and the fresh air rushed in.

"Are you sure?" Theo knew if anyone killed either his mother or brother, they would pay with their lives. If something happened to James, he wasn't sure what he would do.

James nodded. "I'm sure. Besides, sometimes we have to put the past behind us and look to the future. I've got a really bright future to look forward to because you're part of it."

"Mom and Fynn are your family now, too," Theo said. "I know it's not the same as your own, but at least you're not alone anymore."

"Never again." James walked over to the edge of the roof. "So did Naya tell you what was decided?"

Theo shook his head. He had a lot of trouble keeping his curiosity about it under wraps. "Just that we have to go back to Santa Fe. But not why."

"That's because I asked to be the one to tell you." Eluna stalked out onto the roof with a guard shadowing her.

James ducked his head and smiled ruefully. "I thought it would be better to hear it from the man he loves."

"Naturally you would. But official business should be handled officially." Eluna turned her attention to Theo. "In light of the deaths involved, and per the request of several high ranking Enforcers, it is the decision of the Council for both you and Fynn to be drafted into the Enforcers. Effective immediately, which is why another trip to Santa Fe is in order."

The news hit Theo like a brick. He'd never really considered long-term career paths, but if he had, being an Enforcer would've been the last thing on his list. Not because he wasn't interested, but because he'd always thought of Enforcers as a certain class of shifter, and, well, he didn't see himself as anything but low class. As the turmoil in his mind kicked into high gear, James stepped up beside him and laid a hand on his shoulder.

"Don't let it overwhelm you. Since they've requested my skills to teach the next group of recruits, I've requested in return for you two to be in the initial round. They even approved for me to teach from my cabin." James spoke calmly, as if he knew Theo bordered on panic and sought to soothe his mate.

Granted the idea of a class being taught from James' cabin made Theo laugh, so James succeeded in a way. "How on earth are you going to house the recruits in your little cabin?"

One dark brow arched on James' forehead. "Oh ye of little faith. Actually, I was hoping you'd lend a hand in building a bunk house. Once the Enforcers get me the money to get it done."

Theo glanced over at Eluna, who patiently waited with her hands clasped in front of her.

"Are there any other stipulations to your decision?" Theo felt like the other shoe hadn't dropped yet, and wanted to get it over with.

Eluna smiled warmly. "I know you're an intelligent young man. I hope your brother follows your example." She cleared her throat. "There is a small request I have of a more personal nature."

Crossing his arms, Theo leaned into James and waited.

The wizened woman nodded, looked down to blink a few times, and looked back up. "You have to be the one to break the news to your mother. I'm sure she'll have stipulations of her own, which I'm sure we can accommodate, but that woman can be quite terrifying when she wants to be."

For a moment Theo thought Eluna was making a joke, but the crease in the middle of her forehead made him think otherwise. He couldn't help his smile or the bubbling laughter that took its time bursting forward to break the silence. "I don't blame you for being intimidated, really I don't. Okay, I'll be the one to tell my mother."

Eluna heaved an exaggerated sigh and stepped forward with her arms held out. "Welcome to our ranks, Theo Montoya. The shifter world at large needs more people like you."

Theo accepted her hug, breathing deep of her cinnamon and vanilla scent. "I'll work hard to live up to the title."

Naya arrived shortly after, and Theo worried about her making the trip to the airport. Before shifting, she assured him the short distance would be simple enough, and promised to nap the rest of the trip to Santa Fe.

James flew close to Theo, allowing Naya to take point, and brushed his wing tips against various parts of Theo's eagle form. He wasn't sure how his mother or brother would take the news, but he felt confident they were all flying toward a brighter future.

Chapter Twenty

THE TRUCK backed into James' drive, with Theo directing the driver so as not to hit any trees. The lumber for the new bunk house teetered on the bed and only stayed in place because of the railings. James watched with a dry lump in his throat. He'd let Theo take care of most of the people interaction, even though Burt had arranged for shifter-friendly deliveries.

Rubbing his arms, James looked at the large concrete slab now dominating the south slope of the hill leading to his home. Preparations were coming along faster than expected, and though he looked forward to starting classes with a mix of nerves and anticipation, James couldn't help but feel a pang for the loss of his freedom.

"Fynn! Get your butt out here and help unload the two by fours!" Theo's shout brought James out of his silent worries.

"Hang on! I have to finish my Skype with Mom!" Fynn yelled back from inside James' cabin.

Both their presence and enthusiasm had gone a long way toward healing the new scars on James' heart. He'd contacted old family friends and confirmed that his family had all died in a mysterious fire shortly after his own supposed demise. The friends were quick enough to accept that James was an old college buddy of the Chan's dearly departed son, and spoke of both himself and his family fondly. He'd thanked them for their warmth and then practically climbed into Theo's lap as soon as he hung up the phone.

Fynn came running out of the cabin, all long limbs and overly big clothes flapping about. "Thanks, Mom said I had to get my behind out here and help, or she'd come up here and give me a good whipping!"

"Well I guess you'd better get to gettin' if you don't want her to make good on her promise." Theo threw a pair of work gloves at his brother.

"Okay, okay. It's bad enough she's making me do homework before school even starts. I'd rather be training. Do I have to go home for dumb old school? Can't I just test out since I'm going to be an Enforcer?" He slipped his thin hands into the big gloves and kind of resembled Goofy when he placed his fists on his hips.

"Hey, don't look at me. I'm not getting in the middle of the agreement between Mom and Eluna. No way." Theo helped the driver pull the side railing off before moving to the back one. He glanced over at James and smiled.

Warmth spread like a small fire in James' middle. He loved that smile.

"James, you'd vouch for me, right?" Fynn pouted his full bottom lip out, his dark eyes big in his youthful face.

Just like Theo, Fynn would be a handful for whatever poor soul took him on as a mate. James couldn't help but smile as he shook his head furiously.

"Heck to the no! Your mom gets what she wants. End of story."

"Ugh, you two are so lame." Fynn busied himself unloading lumber, grumbling about how he would be much cooler when he got old.

James snorted and headed toward the sound of an oncoming car. There were only a few things expected to arrive, and the big one was already there. So that left a new arrival. He avoided the side of the truck being worked out of and came around the front of the hood as an Uber pulled into the remaining space available in his drive.

A young man, maybe twenty, hopped out of the sliding door with a rucksack in hand. He handed the driver something and closed the door, giving the roof a firm pat before the driver began backing up. Dark blue-black hair swept down into a face that could've been some kind of Pacific Islander or possibly Filipino in origin, but James couldn't be sure.

"Hey, I'm Blayze. Blayze Pascual." He held out his hand to James.

Taking it firmly, James shook Blayze's hand and tried to formulate a proper greeting for an instructor to a new student. He came up blank.

"This is James Chan, your instructor for the foreseeable future. And I'm Theo Montoya, fellow student and James' mate." Theo walked up and offered his own hand.

James had to focus on letting go so Theo and Blayze could shake. His mouth felt thick all of a sudden.

"So you're the legendary eagle with the gift of foresight who faked his death. I tell you, a lot of shifters from my hometown spoke about you in hushed tones. Guess I wasn't expecting you to look so green around the gills." Blayze laughed as he tried to break the ice with humor.

"I don't think I'll ever be fully prepared to be a teacher. Handling a werewolf pack seems so much easier, and frankly, so was doling out justice." He smiled, but Blayze swallowed hard in response to what James had thought would be an appropriate joke.

"Don't worry, Blayze. You're not a werewolf, so I think you're safe for now." Theo gave James a mock stern glare. "How about I introduce you to my brother and we can go from there?"

With Theo leading the way, James followed Blayze around the truck. Fynn set down an armload of lumber and turned back toward them before stopping in his tracks.

"Hey! A new kid! Great, someone not so old for a change." He dusted his hands and jogged over.

"Someone needs to tell him we're not old." James said to Theo.

"I'll get my mom right on that." Theo laughed.

Blayze simply assessed the other boy as he jogged. "Old people aren't so bad. You know, sometimes they have some cool stories to tell."

Skidding to a stop, Fynn look fit to burst with exasperation. "Aw, come on, I thought I had someone on my side for once."

"I think it's too soon to be choosing sides. How about we start with something a little more in common.

The three of us are all eagles. What kind of bird are you Blayze?" Theo asked.

James made a note to talk to Theo about helping with lessons in the future. He seemed to be pretty good with speaking to strangers.

"Well, it would be easier to simply show you. I'm not a large bird of prey like you all. But, well, you'll see." Blayze set his bag down and started stripping off clothing.

Fynn averted his gaze. He was still young and probably not used to shifting around anyone but his brother.

Once Blayze freed himself from the restrictive clothing, he took two steps and shifted. A small bird flapped its wings where the young man stood only moments before. He had the shape of a bluejay, but the only white visible was two small swooshes above the eyes. His head was black and there were black flight feathers on his wings, but the rest of him sported bright blue plumage. He was quite beautiful.

"Wow! A Steller's Jay! Cool, I've never seen one in person." Fynn shaded his eyes and watched the bird wing his way through the tree limbs.

Surprised, James looked to Theo for an explanation, but Theo merely shrugged. Apparently James had to put all preconceived notions aside, and prepare himself to accept that wonders never ceased. The thought reminded James that he needed to talk to Theo alone.

"Hey, Theo?" James asked softly.

Theo turned back as Fynn followed Blayze toward the tree line. Together the two of them flew high into the open skies above them. Not a cloud, physical or otherwise hung over the clearing. A warm smile tugged on his full lips, making James wish he could simply kiss him instead of speaking the next words.

"Look, I wanted to talk to you when we were alone. While Fynn is distracted, I want you to know that I've been using my renewed resources to dig up some info…" James hesitated there, still not wanting to upset Theo.

He stepped closer to James, cupping his cheek. "Hey, it's okay. Whatever you have to say can't be all that bad."

Deciding to just get it over with, James blurted, "I found your father."

The End

The Enforcers continues 2020 in
"Blackfeather on the Wind"
If you enjoyed Open Skies please leave a review on
your favorite bookseller site.

About the Authors

A.J. Marcus

A.J. has been writing to pass the time since high school. The stories he wrote helped him deal with life. A few years ago, he started sharing those stories with friends who enjoyed them and he has started sending his works out into the world to share with other people. He lives in the mountains with his extremely supportive husband. They have a lot of critters, including dogs, cats, birds, horses, and rabbits. When not writing, A.J. spends a lot of time hiking, trail riding, or just driving in the mountains. Nature provides a lot of inspiration for his work and keeps him writing. He is also an avid photographer and falconer. Don't get him started talking about his birds because he won't stop for a while.

Web Contact Info:
Website: www.ajmarcus.com
Email: andy@ajmarcus.com
Twitter: twitter.com/#!/aj_marcus
Facebook: http://
www.facebook.com/authorajmarcus

Nicole Godfrey

Nicole Godfrey calls the beautiful city of Colorado Springs home, along with her furry children. She was born in Omaha, Nebraska, and has lived in Florida and Tennessee. Her writing career started with poetry at a young age, leading to her first publication at the age of twelve. Poetry eventually evolved into the love of storytelling, and any good story, no matter the genre, is open to her creative mind. She has two short stories published through Colorado Springs Fiction Writers Group: "A Page Lost" in *An Uncommon Collection* and "The Power of the Word" in *Remnants and Resolutions: Tales of Survival*.

When she's not writing, Nicole actively participates in Amtgard and loves to play tabletop RPGs. Art has also been a part of her life since a young age, so she spends as much time as possible playing with different mediums.

A winner of NaNoWriMo and PPWC scholarship recipient, Nicole strives to become a better writer every day.

You can reach her at:
E-mail: authornicolegodfrey@gmail.com

Other Books you might find interesting:

Chasing the waves

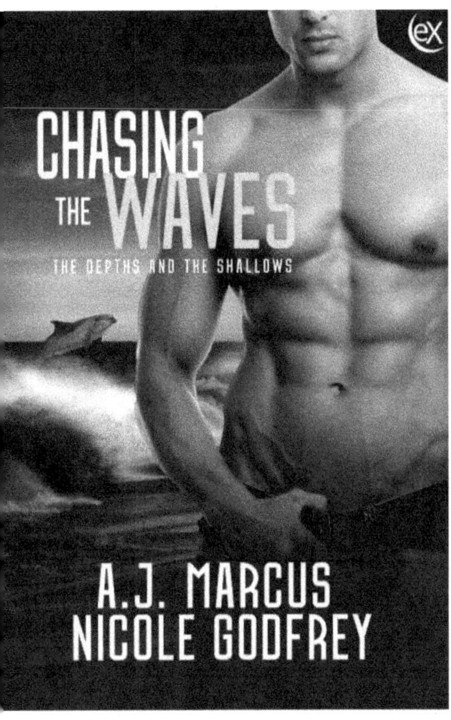

Can a dolphin shifter and a human survive the sharks long enough to find the love they are both so desperate for?

As an agent of The Shallows, Galadir accepts a job escorting a family of Selkies from Tasmania to Ireland, knowing there will be risk, but there are lots of sharks and other operatives of The Depths, an organization of shifters bent on reclaiming the oceans for themselves, bent on stopping them. When things get dire, Galadir is forced to accept aid from an unexpected source.

Chase Crowely is a marine photographer who has just got his first assignment from a major nature magazine and he races around the world to try to photograph the unusual sight of a dolphin protecting fur seals. Little does he know there's much more to the story than he suspects and by the time he gets the pictures he wants, he's torn between his need to complete the assignment and his need to protect his new love.

The two unlikely men come together to protect others, at the possibility of destroying their own lives or at the very least their hearts.

Hoofbeats

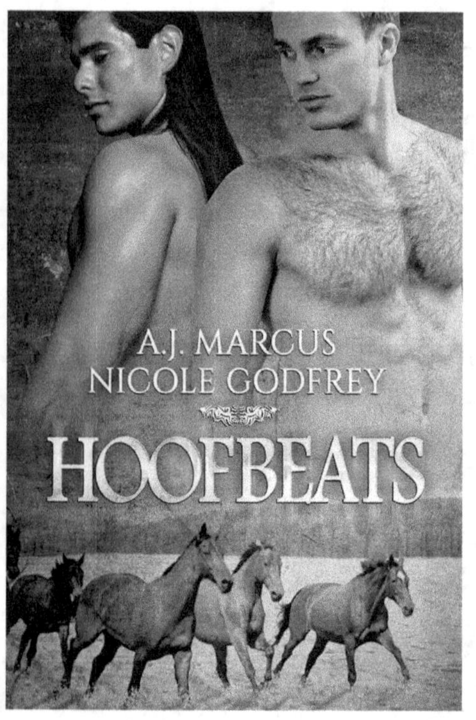

After a run of bad luck, gifted horse trainer Cole Frasier thinks he's lost his touch. When he's offered three times his normal rate to gentle a stallion, he needs the money badly enough he jumps at the opportunity, even if his boss is of questionable morality.

Once he meets Midnight Blood, he knows there's something special about the horse, but he doesn't know how special until he begins sharing dreams with the magnificent steed.

Derek Dancing Hawk is a horse shifter trapped in his horse form due to guilt over losing the wild herd he was guarding. When he meets Cole, as Midnight Blood, he wants to find a way to be human again. During a fight between Cole and the ranch foreman, he manages to shift and save Cole, but his transformation from horse to human is captured on camera. This not only gives Cole's boss blackmail material, but also creates the need to warn the horse shifter council of the threat to their anonymity. The existence of shifters is a closely guarded secret; one they will go to great lengths to keep.

The Kachina Job

The lion, the jaguar, and the owl against the werewolf. Who will prevail?

Phillip Twohands is a thief and a weremountain lion. When he takes a job stealing an ugly kachina, he never realizes it will change his life forever. Daniel Hernandez is a werejaguar who is hired to steal the same kachina by the same werewolf who hired Phillip. When their paths cross, it becomes clear the tension between them is not all about rivalry.

The local sheriff, Shannon O'Flaherty, catches them in the act and has no choice but to take the two into his personal custody, which quickly ends up with the three of them in bed together.

When they learn the kachina has an ancient wolf spirit trapped inside, they rally to prevent it from transferring its power to the werewolf who hired them, but it will take all the strength in their new bond to succeed.

Power Play

Naga Industries wasn't Calvin's first choice of a place to intern. It wasn't even his tenth. But when every other internship spot is taken, he finds himself at the mercy of Draeke Lindwurm and he's way over his head.

Draeke doesn't want an intern, but his go-to man is threatening to revolt if he doesn't get them both some help. Calvin is everything Draeke doesn't like in men. He's too young, too average, never on time, doesn't dress well, and worst of all Calvin is human which makes things complicated between them when he becomes a pawn in a power play with the world's dragon elite.